CHANDLER: CIRCLE CITY FRAME

CHANDLER: CIRCLE CITY FRAME

Bill Craig

ABSOLUTELY AMAZING eBOOKS

ABSOLUTELY AMAZING eBOOKS

Published by Whiz Bang LLC, 926 Truman Avenue, Key West, Florida 33040, USA.

For information contact:
Publisher@AbsolutelyAmazingEbooks.com

ISBN-13: 978-1945772535 (Absolutely Amazing Ebooks)

ISBN-10: 1945772530

To my Children with love. I know I am not the easiest person to get to know, but to those who have made the effort, this one is for you!

Other books in this series:

Circle City Shakedown
Circle City Slam

CHANDLER:
CIRCLE CITY
FRAME

Chapter One

Indianapolis, Indiana.

Arnie Grossman groaned as he opened his eyes. His head was killing him. It felt like somebody was using it to split firewood with a dull axe. He rolled out of his bed and barely made it to the bathroom before throwing up. He emptied his stomach into the toilet. After three minutes, he wiped his mouth with toilet paper and tossed it into the bowl before finding the flush handle and depressing it. The water swirled and took the mess down the drain before refilling.

Arnie felt like he had been sucker-punched by Mike Tyson. He could barely remain upright as he made his way out of the bedroom. He turned on the lights in the living room. He froze as the lights came up. A woman lay on the floor in a pool of blood.

She looked familiar. She was young, barely out of her teens from the look of her. She had shoulder-length brown hair, pale brown skin, wide brown eyes stared lifelessly from her face. She had been well put together and he remembered she exuded a sensual aura of compact sexuality. Her name was Tiffany; at least that was the name she had given him down in the bar earlier in the evening. His stomach heaved, even though there was nothing left inside it. Arnie stumbled back into the bedroom and dug his cell phone out of his pocket.

What was that private eye's name? Oh yeah, Chandler. Arnie scrolled through his contacts until he found the number. He pressed call. It rang twice before a male voice answered. "Chandler."

"Mr. Chandler? This is Arnie Grossman. We met at that thing for the Indianapolis Stallions? I need your help and I need it right now," Arnie said.

"Where are you, Mr. Grossman?" Chandler asked. Grossman gave him his address. It was up in Fishers. "Give me about forty-five minutes, Mr. Grossman. Maybe less depending on traffic." Chandler hung up and Grossman laid his phone back on the nightstand next to the bed. Arnie slipped his feet into his loafers. Forty-five minutes with the dead girl in his living room was going to seem like an eternity. He headed for the kitchen to make coffee.

~ ~ ~

"What was that all about?" Mary Norman, his lover and secretary asked, sitting up in the bed they shared. The covers slipped off to reveal two perfect breasts. Chandler had already pulled on pants and shoes and was pulling a black T-shirt over his head.

"It sounds like a new case," Phillip Chandler replied. He was around six feet tall and slender with short dark hair and blue eyes. There was a scar next to his left eye, a souvenir from his days as a Deputy U.S. Marshal. He walked over to the dresser and slipped on his shoulder holster that held his Colt Commander .45 with finger-grooved Hogue grips and tritium three dot night sights. There were two spare magazines under the off side of the holster.

"Does this new case have a name?" Mary asked as she threw off the covers and found her fluffy blue terrycloth housecoat. She pulled it around her tiny frame and tied the belt. Barefoot, she opened the bedroom door and Simba, the yellow tabby that had adopted Chandler, padded inside and rubbed against her legs purring loudly. Mary knelt and stroked his head, making him purr louder. "Men," she smiled as she stood and headed for the kitchen to start coffee.

Chandler had snagged his brown leather bomber jacket from the closet on the way out of the bedroom. "You weren't complaining earlier as I recall," he grinned at her.

"That was before I got woke up by a ringing telephone," Mary told him.

"Touché," he replied.

"So, does this new client have a name?"

"He does. His name is Arnie, nee Arnold Grossman. He's a businessman and philanthropist whose name had been in the Indianapolis Star a lot lately. While I go meet with him, why don't you see what you can dig up on him on-line?" Chandler suggested. He grabbed a bottle of water from the fridge and headed for the door to the garage.

"Will do," Mary called after him before the door into the garage closed. Mary started the coffee and then headed for the living room and the laptop that she carried back and forth from the office. She had come a long way from her days as a dancer at the Red Garter where she had worked under the name of Mary Blue. That was how she and Chandler had met. She had hired him to find a friend, another dancer that had disappeared after going to work a private party.[1]

---

[1]

It seemed like a lifetime ago, though it had only been a couple of years. Time had a way of flying when times were good. She took a seat on the couch and booted the computer up.

~ ~ ~

Normally to get from his house in Beech Grove to Grossman's house would take thirty-six minutes, but at three o'clock in the morning, he made it in twenty. Chandler parked his dark green Jeep Cherokee in the driveway of the imposing structure. Grossman's house looked like it had to have at least five bedrooms. Compared to the one bedroom bungalow that she shared with Mary and Simba, this place was a mansion. The front porch light was on and Chandler made his way to the front door and rang the bell. It didn't take but a few seconds for Arnie Grossman to answer. The man looked like hell, his dark hair disheveled, his eyes red. The odors of sweat, alcohol, and vomit wafted off of him in a thick cloud. The white shirt he had on was wrinkled and looked like it had been slept in as did his pants.

"Chandler?" he asked, his voice sounding weak and raspy.

"That's me."

"Please come in, I need your help," he said, leading the way. He stopped in the living room. Half a heartbeat later, Chandler saw why.

"Have you called the police?" Chandler asked, looking at the dead body of the young woman.

"No. I called you as soon as I found her."

Chandler: Circle City Shakedown.

"Do you know her name?"

"Her name was Tiffany, at least that's what she told me at the bar," Grossman said.

"Which bar and when?" Chandler asked.

"I don't remember."

"Arnie, I need you to tell me everything. Start at the beginning."

"My head hurts really bad, but I'll try," Grossman said.

~ ~ ~

Twenty minutes later, Chandler called the police to report a murder had taken place. Fishers had a small department of its own, but for a homicide they would likely call in the Indianapolis Metro Homicide division. But their own Criminal Investigation Division would arrive on the scene and make that call. Chandler had no problem with that. He was pretty sure that Arnie Grossman had nothing to do with the killing of the young woman that lay on his living room floor. Chandler also placed a call to a doctor friend who had agreed to be there in fifteen minutes.

The doctor was going to come and draw a blood sample from Arnie Grossman. Chandler was already pretty sure of what the results of that blood draw would show. Then he dialed Mary as he poured himself a cup of coffee in Grossman's kitchen.

"How bad is it?" Mary asked when she picked up.

"As bad as it gets. Arnie woke up to find the dead body of a girl he had met earlier in the evening at some club, he doesn't remember which one. Based on his eyes and the headache he described, I think Arnie was roofied," Chandler told her.

"Somebody isn't happy with him at all," Mary whistled.

"I'd guess not. The local cops are on the way, but I'm pretty sure they will kick this over to the Metro Homicide division."

"That sounds like a good bet. Your friend Arnie has been spreading a lot of cash around town, but he's also been making some enemies too. He's bankrolled at least three community centers in high crime areas and has helped kids get involved with sports instead of gangs. The gang leaders are less than pleased with him."

"Are they pissed enough to frame him for murder?"

"I don't know, but you might well be asking them if you decided to pursue this," Mary told him.

"'You know I will," Chandler told her.

"Yes, I do. I'm willing to bet I won't see you until you come into the office?"

'That's probably a good bet. Could you give Larry Sampson a call and let him know what is going on? I think Arnie is going to need him," Chandler told her.

"I can do that, Love. You owe me a nice lunch since I gave up half a night's sleep for this," Mary told him, smiling.

"Yes, I do. You pick the place and I'll pick you up at the office around 11:30 this morning."

"See you then," Mary said, breaking the connection. She dialed Larry Simpson's number. She didn't like the weasel-faced attorney but she had to admit that he was very good at his job.

~ ~ ~

Nick Havershaw frowned as he rolled up on the address. It was in one of the wealthier neighborhoods, and to Havershaw looked like a damned mansion. He had been home and fast asleep, cuddled up to his wife when the Chief had called and told him to get over Arnie Grossman's place right away. Calls to homes of people of Grossman's stature were never a good sign. It could mean anything from an overdose to a robbery.

He opened his door and climbed out of the car, taking a long moment to stretch before reaching back inside for his evidence collection bag. Nick started the long walk from where he was parked to the main house. The Coroner's wagon was already there as well as crime scene techs. The Chief had mentioned a homicide and said the Indianapolis Metro would probably be sending over a pair of their homicide detectives, but until they arrived, Havershaw was in charge.

A uniform met him at the front door and had him sign in on an access form on a plastic clipboard. Havershaw showed his ID, signed the form and then stepped inside. The techs were hard at work, but had laid out a safety zone where people could walk inside the large living room. Carol Nevis had just finished with the body and a couple of her assistants were zipping it into a body bag to take the victim back to the morgue. "What have we got, Carol?"

"It was a homicide for sure. If it was more than that, well, I'll have to wait until I have her on the table to know. But somebody shot her in the back of the skull, probably with a .22 since there was no exit wound," the part-time Coroner told him as she peeled off her latex gloves and dropped them in a small plastic bag she carried with her.

"Do we have a time of death?"

"Approximately 2 a.m. give or take thirty minutes," Nevis shrugged.

"Okay, that's good to know. Any idea where I can find the home owner, this Grossman guy?" Havershaw asked.

"You might try the kitchen," Nevis told him before she picked up her bag and headed for the door.

"Thanks," Havershaw called after her. He headed for the kitchen, letting the tech people do their thing. Two men were seated at the kitchen table, mugs of coffee sitting in front of them. One was tall and rumpled looking, with thinning red hair, and a pudgy looking face and belly. The other man was tall and slender, but it was obvious that he worked out. He had black hair, blue eyes and a cold look about him. He was dressed in black except for a brown leather bomber jacket.

"Which one of you is Grossman?" Havershaw asked. The rumpled man looked up, blinking his eyes.

"Me," he said.

"And you are?" Havershaw directed his gaze at the man in black.

"Phillip Chandler. I'm an investigator whose services were retained by Mister Grossman. I am here to protect his rights until his lawyer arrives," Chandler replied in a bored tone. While they had never met, Havershaw knew Chandler by his reputation.

"Who is Mr. Grossman's attorney?"

"Larry Sampson," Chandler replied. Havershaw winced as he heard the name. Sampson was one of the top criminal lawyers in the state. This case was getting more complicated by the moment.

"Since we don't have a homicide division, my boss

has arranged to hand this over to Indy metro Homicide. They should be arriving very soon," Havershaw told them, suddenly glad to be handing this mess off.

"That's good to know," Chandler replied, never taking his eyes off Havershaw.

Chapter Two

Detective Alejandro Cruz groaned when he walked in the door and spotted Phillip Chandler. The pair had a rocky relationship, but they did make an effective team. "What the hell, Chandler?" Cruz asked.

"You might want to talk to Detective Havershaw first," Chandler told him, enjoying the other man's discomfort. Larry Sampson picked that moment to walk through the door. Larry was barely five feet tall, bald on top with black hair making a fringe around his skull. His suit looked like a sausage skin that had been packed too tight.

"Ah, Detective Cruz, how nice to see you again. May I have a few minutes with Mr. Grossman?" Larry asked, an amused glint in his eyes.

"Sure thing, but I have to let you know that he hasn't been read his rights yet," Cruz replied.

"All the better," Sampson nodded. With that, Cruz and Havershaw exited the kitchen, leaving it to the lawyer, Chandler and Grossman. "So, would one of you care to fill me in?" Sampson looked at the pair.

~ ~ ~

"Arnie called me and said he was in trouble. I came over and saw that he was. I called Mary and had her call you," Chandler shrugged. He leaned against the wall looking bored but in reality, was anything but. His eyes missed nothing as they looked the kitchen over.

"Did you know the dead woman?" Sampson asked.

"I met her earlier this evening, one of the clubs over in Broad Ripple I think. I don't remember a whole hell of a lot," Grossman said dejectedly.

"You had been drinking a lot?"

"Yes. Way more than I should have been, but I was celebrating a deal being put together that would put four new community centers on the East Side."

"A worthy cause for celebration for sure. Were you indulging in any other recreational substances besides alcohol?"

"Not knowingly."

"Dr. Kimble should be here soon, and he's going to do a blood draw. It will determine current alcohol levels in your blood as well as any other substances that might have been introduced into your drinks."

"Okay, Mr. Sampson," Grossman nodded, wincing at the sudden stabbing pain in his skull.

"Phillip, what do you need to get started on this?" Sampson looked at Chandler.

"I need a good picture of our client, plus I'll need access to his office and computers, names of friends and family members who might have been with him at the celebration," Chandler replied. "Oh, and a retainer check would be nice."

"Come by my office at ten and I'll take care of your retainer. Do you have a good photo Mr. Grossman? One that Phillip can use to try and verify your story?" Sampson asked his client.

"Yes, there is a picture with me and the mayor on the mantle above the fireplace."

"Phillip?"

"I'll get it. Have Larry write you a receipt for it," Chandler stood and moved back out into the living room, staying in the safe zone as he made his way to the mantle and took the picture. He carried it back to the kitchen, frame and all.

Chandler watched as his client removed the picture from the frame with shaky hands and handed it to him. Chandler rolled it up and put it in the inside pocket of his bomber jacket. At that point, Dr. Richard Kimball entered the room. Kimball was an older man with a thick mane of dark hair that was starting to show some white at the temples, giving him a distinguished look.

"Richard, thank you for coming over. This is Mr. Grossman, my client. Please draw enough to do a full toxicology screen. I suspect that he might well have been drugged earlier in the evening, or last night as the case appears to be since the sun is now starting to rise," Sampson explained.

"Not a problem, Larry. You know I'm always happy to help," Kimball replied, setting his medical bag on the table.

~ ~ ~

"So, are you ready to tell me what this is all about?" Detective Cruz asked.

"I wish I knew, Alejandro. I got a call in the middle of the night to come over here. I called Larry to represent him. That really is all I know right now," Chandler told the detective.

"I wish I could believe you, Chandler."

"Hey, I'm telling you the truth. You know exactly as much about this case as I do."

"We shall see," Cruz replied.

"Either way, I am done here for the night. Larry will go with him downtown. Have a good night, Cruz," Chandler told him as he headed for the door. He climbed into his Jeep and headed back to Beech Grove. The sky was already light and almost blue as he headed home.

~ ~ ~

So, what did you find out?" Mary asked as he entered the kitchen.

"Not a lot, but I don't think that Grossman committed murder," Chandler told her.

"That is something at least," Mary shook her head.

"It is, but the big question is, is it enough?" Chandler asked her.

"I wish I knew," Mary told him.

"So do I. I want you to head to the office. I'll be around later."

"How much later?"

"I don't know yet. I want to grab a shower and shave, and then go talk to some of Grossman's pals. I'm hoping that they might be able to tell me more about his party last night," Chandler explained.

"That sounds like a good idea," Mary smiled at him.

"I thought so," he nodded.

~ ~ ~

Doctor Richard Kimble was back at his office. Based on what Grossman had told him about how he was feeling when he woke up and the several hour gap in his memory, Kimble was sure that Grossman had been slipped a drug, probably something like Ketamine, or maybe rohypnol. Kimble frowned. For someone to drug

Arnie Grossman, it suggested that they wanted him either locked up or discredited from being a witness about something. He would have to mention that to Larry.

~ ~ ~

Arnie Grossman sat dejectedly in a white-walled room with a large mirror hanging on the wall. Arnie knew, as did anybody that had ever watched a cop show, that the mirror was made of one-way glass, so that other cops could watch his interrogation. Still, when the door opened, Arnie was sure glad to see Larry Sampson enter the room. Sampson looked cool and confident as he walked around the table and took a seat next to Arnie.

"Can you get me out of this?" Arnie asked.

"That is a big question, Arnie. A young woman was just found dead inside your house." Larry Sampson explained.

"I know that. I found her, remember?" Grossman rolled his eyes.

"Arnie, the detectives are going to be in her to question you shortly. If there is anything else you can remember, I need you to tell me everything. You can lie to yourself, lie to the cops, but *never* lie to your attorney."

"I honestly have no idea how she got there. I can't even remember how I got home," Arnie put his face in his hands.

"Then I guess we are going to have to put our faith in Chandler to find out what happened."

~ ~ ~

Mary Norman was dressed in a navy pantsuit and was wearing a pair of Louis Vuitton heels. Her blond hair was pulled up in a ponytail behind her head as she sat at her desk researching Arnie Grossman and the dead girl, whom their client had called Tiffany.

Mary had put her picture on-line and then started running a facial recognition program on the picture. She was sure that it might take days to get a match. Still, it was what Phil would want her to do. She wondered what her boss/boyfriend was doing while she was doing this check. She had no doubt that it was something that Chandler would want to know.

~ ~ ~

Alejandro Cruz smiled as he eyed Arnie Grossman through the one-way glass in the interrogation room. Grossman was a physical wreck, sweating, shaky, looking like he was just coming down off a bad trip. Cruz wondered how long the guy was going to play at claiming not to remember anything. Just more sauce for the goose. Cruz scooped up the file that had pictures of the dead girl and headed into the interrogation room.

Cruz was around six feet tall, well built and muscular with dark brown hair and Hispanic good looks. Brown eyes looked out of a handsome face. A dark mustache covered his upper lip. He was wearing a dark blue suit with a pale blue tie and black cordovans. He looked more like a businessman than a cop.

Cruz didn't speak as he pulled out a chair and sat down across from Grossman. Larry Sampson sat in a chair next to his client. Cruz lifted his eyes to look at both men before opening the folder on the table.

"Do you understand why you were arrested, Mr. Grossman?" Cruz asked.

"I woke up to a dead woman in my house,"

Grossman said woodenly.

"Can you tell me how she got there?"

"I have no idea," Grossman mumbled.

"You have no idea? Yet you were able to tell the first officers on the scene the victim's first name. Were you trying to be intimate with her and things went bad? It's happened before with you rich cats," Cruz said.

"I don't know. The last thing I remember was being at a party in Broad Ripple, I don't even know how I got home," Grossman sighed.

"Don't leave town, Mr. Grossman, this investigation is far from over."

"Are you allowing my client to leave, Detective?" Sampson asked.

"For now. His house is off limits until our boys from the Crime Scene Unit are done. But keep me notified as to his whereabouts," Cruz replied.

~ ~ ~

Morning was not a time to find anybody at the clubs, as most were closed until much later in the afternoon. He headed for Larry Sampson's office. He figured that the attorney would be done at the police station by now. He hoped that Grossman might be able to provide a list of the people that he had gone out to celebrate with.

Chandler's cell phone started ringing so he pulled over to the curb and parked before pulling it out and answering. It was Doc Kimble. "Doctor Kimble, what have you got?"

"Arnie Grossman was roofied," Kimble replied.

"Interesting. That certainly explains why he can't remember anything," Chandler noted.

"Yes, it does. I'm about to call Mr. Sampson and let him know as well. I figured you should know first," Dr. Kimble replied.

"Thanks, Doc. I appreciate it," Chandler ended the call and headed for the attorney's office once more. Now that he knew that Grossman was drugged, it would help him in his inquires to find out who might have had both the motive and the opportunity to do it.

Chapter Three

Sampson wasn't back in his office yet, so Chandler headed for the office. He was hungry and figured Mary would be too. He wondered where she would choose to go eat. He parked near the office and walked the block to where the office was located in a second-floor walk-up over another attorney's office just a couple of blocks away from the building where the Social Security Disability hearings were held.

The overhead was higher but having an actual office rather than a table at the Slippery Noodle had brought in enough clients to afford it and to pay Mary an actual salary for acting as his secretary/assistant. Yes, they were lovers, but Chandler didn't want her to feel obligated if she ever wanted to move on.

Mary was on the phone when Chandler entered, so he headed into his inner office. After showering and shaving earlier he had changed into a white shirt, black tie, and light gray suit. He also wore black socks and shoes.

He was going through the stack of mail on his desk when Mary walked in. "That was Larry, he said he would fax over a list of people that were with Arnie last night by four this afternoon."

"Good, I'm going to need that list before I can do much else on Arnie's case. Where would you like to go to eat lunch?" Chandler asked her.

"How about Taste of Havana? I hear they serve

authentic Cuban cuisine," Mary said.

"It's been a while since I've had Cuban food. The last time it happened, I was working a case as a Deputy Marshal down in Key West, chasing after a terrorist," Chandler replied.

"Did you catch him?"

"We did."

On the way out, Mary turned on the answering machine and Chandler locked the door behind them. They walked to his Cherokee and got in. Chandler pulled out into the street heading for Broad Ripple Avenue.

Taste of Havana was located in a small storefront, the outside painted gray with yellow trim and the address painted in black. The sign with the name was black with a black alligator trimmed in yellow alongside the name. Chandler opened the door for Mary and escorted her inside. There were tables on the walk outside, but the sky was gray and threatening so Mary had opted to eat inside.

The floor was white and the interior walls were painted a bright yellow, orange, and green. There were white wooden picnic tables as well as traditional wooden tables and padded chairs. A young Cuban woman came to take their order. Her nametag read Dayana. Mary ordered the Old Cloth, shredded beef, slow cooked in sofrito sauce with julienned onions, peppers and white wine served with black beans, served with white rice, and a side of sweet plantains. Chandler opted for an El Cubano sandwich and they both ordered Cuban coffee.

"A sandwich? I had figured that you would opt to

impress me by ordering something more exotic," Mary smiled across the table at him.

"I could have, but their Cubano sandwiches are awesome."

"You've eaten here before?"

"I have, before we met. It was right after I moved to Indianapolis, before I set up shop at the Slippery Noodle," Chandler shrugged.

"But you said you hadn't eaten Cuban food since Key West," it was not a question.

"Well, I didn't actually eat the food here. I ordered it as carry out."

"Semantics, love. Don't play games with me," Mary told him.

"You are the only person that I don't play games with," Chandler reminded her.

"Good to know. So, what are your plans for the rest of the day?"

"I plan on going through the rest of the mail until Larry faxes us the list. Once we have it, I plan on running those names down and seeing what they can tell me about last night," Chandler told her.

"That does suspiciously like a good plan of action," Mary admitted.

"I have my moments," Chandler grinned.

"Yes, you do," Mary smiled and he felt his pulse start to race. The waitress returned with their food, and soon they were busy eating.

~ ~ ~

Alejandro Cruz was at the IU Medical Center Morgue for the autopsy of the dead woman. She had been transferred to the Metro morgue as well since it was now a metro Homicide case. The only name they had for the poor girl was Tiffany. That at least was better than Jane Doe.

Lauren Donner was doing the autopsy. Lauren was a petite woman, barely topping the five foot three mark. She had short blonde hair cut in a pixie cut. She had blue eyes that were hidden behind dark-framed glasses and a Plexiglas face shield. She wore light green scrubs and a paper bonnet covered her hair and her shoes. Blue latex gloves covered her hands. She picked up a scalpel and made a y-incision on the torso. This would expose both the chest cavity and the abdominal cavity.

"Couldn't you start with her skull?" Cruz asked, feeling slightly green around the gills. He hated attending autopsies.

"No, I can't. Autopsies follow a definite and precise pattern so that nothing will be missed, Detective," Lauren Donner replied.

"She was shot in the head," Cruz reminded her. To him, that seemed the obvious place to start cutting.

"Until I complete the autopsy, I will not sign off on cause of death. There are any number of ways she might have died, and the gunshot wound to the skull was done to confuse the issue." Donner snapped.

"Fine, let me know when you'll be ready to start on the skull," Cruz replied before turning and exiting the autopsy room. He was glad to be outside, away from the smells of blood and formaldehyde. Cruz pulled out his cell phone and called Steve Dickerson, his current partner in homicide.

"Alejandro, how is the autopsy going?" Dickerson asked.

"About like you'd expect. Donner is being as infuriating as ever," Cruz replied.

"Ah, the whole processes are in place for a reason?"

"That's the one."

"Better you than me, Pal. You get anything from your buddy Chandler at the scene?"

"Not really. Grossman called him, he called Larry Sampson to represent Grossman."

"Shit, Larry Sampson? Really?"

"Yes, which is why Grossman is still walking around, instead of sitting in lock-up," Cruz replied.

"Fucking wonderful," Dickerson sighed.

"Tell me about it. You able to find out anything about the girl?"

"Not yet. Her prints weren't in the system."

"I've got a list of names in my pocket from Grossman's mouthpiece. Once I see what Donner has to tell me about the cause of death, I'll come back to the office and start running them," Cruz told him.

"That's something at least."

"Yes, it is."

"I'll see you when you get back," Dickerson said, ending the call. Cruz knew that his partner would continue one of the other homicides that were a part of their caseloads.

~ ~ ~

"That was a very good lunch. We need to eat there more often," Mary told him.

"We do," Chandler agreed.

"You've got something on your mind," Mary observed.

"I do."

"Care to talk about it?"

"Maybe," Chandler nodded. "It isn't anything solid yet."

"Does it have to be for us to discuss it?"

"Not really, no."

"So, start talking," Mary told him.

~ ~ ~

Johnny Quick was sitting in a booth at the Slippery Noodle. He ignored the music, concentrating instead on the tumbler of bourbon in front of him. He had come to Indianapolis a couple of years before. His job had been to erase a young pro basketball player who had decided not to shave points. Somebody else had set the kid up for the murder of his fiancé.

Quick had liked the kid, knew he was a talented basketball player. So, he had gone against the mob boss that he worked for and decided to help get the kid out of trouble. That was how he had met Phillip Chandler. That was how his life had gotten turned upside down. So now he was down in Indianapolis, hiring out as muscle and doing private security gigs to live. He was in demand and he was making good money.

But right now, he was bored. He needed something to do. Something that would get his adrenaline flowing. His cell phone rang. He recognized Chandler's number and decided to answer the call.

"Chandler, to what do I owe the pleasure?" Quick asked.

"I've got an interesting case that I could use some help on," Chandler replied

"You have my attention."

"I thought that I might. Have you heard about the

Grossman murder case?"

"I have. Saw it on the news this morning," Quick replied.

"Grossman is my client. I need to know who he was partying with in Broad Ripple last night," Chandler said.

"I can ask around," Quick nodded to himself.

"I'd appreciate it," Chandler said, before breaking the connection. Johnny Quick smiled as he dropped his cell phone into his pocket. He finished his beer and went to pay his tab, tipping his waitress with a twenty. He put on his dark sunglasses and stepped outside.

Quick was tall and rangy. He had played ball to put himself through college. His head was shaved these days, he was half a step slower, but he could still swish the ball from half court. His face was one that the girls still seemed to like. His dark skin was smooth, the muscles still hard. He worked out daily. He climbed into his Blue Chrysler Crossfire and headed for Broad Ripple.

~ ~ ~

The autopsy was over by the time Chandler reached the morgue. While autopsies didn't really bother him, he took no pleasure in watching a person having the last of their dignity stolen away by doctors trying to find out why they had died. Cruz had already left, and Chandler was glad of that as well. He knocked on Lauren Donner's door and when she said come in, he did, setting a bottle of Wild Turkey on her desk, the seal unbroken.

"A bribe?" Donner looked at him, her cool eyes appraising.

"Call it a gift. I was hoping to hear about the

autopsy on the girl from Grossman's house, without having to suffer through Alejandro Cruz," Chandler told her with a grin.

"I wish that I hadn't had to suffer through him," Donner snorted.

"He's a good detective but he does tend to rub folks the wrong way."

"He's an impatient detective, and impatience makes him sloppy. I can't abide sloppy detectives."

"So, what can you tell me about the girl we know only as Tiffany?"

"She was beaten before she was murdered. Beaten bad enough that a broken rib had punctured her left lung. It was collapsing when somebody pressed the muzzle of a .22 against the side of her head and pulled the trigger. The bullet ricocheted around in there and pureed her brain. I would be willing to bet that the pistol was silenced," Donner explained.

"Professional hit?" Chandler asked.

"If I had to guess, I would say yes. What I can't fathom was why she was murdered in Mr. Grossman's house. Lividity suggests that the body wasn't moved. Also, the paraffin test on Mr. Grossman came up negative, so he was not the shooter," Donner said.

"Yeah, I had a blood draw done on him and he had been doped."

"So, what will you do next?"

"I start hunting for the real killer," Chandler replied.

Mary was busy running computer searches on Arnie Grossman when the fax machine came to life. She hurried over to it, hoping it was the list that Chandler was waiting on. She scanned the document as the machine was spitting it out. Yes, it was the list of people that had been out with Arnie Grossman the night before. She quickly made a copy of it and reached for the phone to let him know that it was in!

Chapter Four

Chandler was heading back to the office when his cell phone rang. He answered it. "What have you got?"

"The list came in. I thought you would want to know," Mary told him.

"That's great! I've got good news too. Grossman wasn't the one that shot the girl."

"That seems like good news."

"It does, except that now we have no clue as to who wants to frame Arnie."

"That is a drawback."

"Yes, it is."

"I should be there in ten minutes. We'll get cracking on this," Chandler replied.

"See you then," Mary said before hanging up. Chandler dropped the phone on the seat beside him as he made his way through the down town traffic. Hopefully the list would give him some place to start in finding out who had tried to frame Arnie Grossman.

~ ~ ~

Johnny Quick sat in his car in a parking lot in front of Land Sharks. This was where the party was supposed to have started. However, it was still several hours before the place opened. He frowned. There had to be somebody he could talk to. He pulled out his phone and started going through his contacts.

~ ~ ~

Ogden Spears, Sarah Luxor, John Irwin, Melody

Williams, Harold Gore, Fabian Morales, Gwen Franks. The list of the people that had been celebrating with Arnie Grossman on Friday night. Chandler recognized a couple of the names, like John Irwin, owner of the Indianapolis Stallions. Ogden Spears owned a construction firm. Chandler looked up at Mary. "How do you want to work this list?" he asked.

"Why don't you work the ladies and I'll take the men? If we don't have any success with that, then we can switch and try it the other way around," Mary smiled at him and it was like the sun coming out from behind a thick cloud.

"That sounds like an equitable split of the workload. I have Johnny Quick looking into things from the other side of the street," Chandler explained.

"You mean the criminal side of things?" Mary arched an eyebrow at him. It was a thing he found incredibly sexy.

"Of course. Crooks can be very talkative among their own," Chandler shrugged.

"I still am not quite sure about how the two of you function together. While from one standpoint, you are polar opposites, but from another, you both are very much alike," Mary said.

"Have you been taking classes on psychology when I wasn't looking?"

"Most of what I know I learned in my former profession as a stripper. It gave me a deep look into the male psyche."

"The whole power and control thing?"

"Exactly. As a woman, I am smaller and less physically powerful, but on the stage, I used my body and charisma to make men want me. I was able to entice them while at the same time retaining a professional distance. I used my sexuality to control them and their responses to me. As you yourself know, I made a good deal of money doing it, but now, I am glad that part of my life is behind me," Mary explained.

"I'm glad that I was able to help you get out. You were far better than the life you were living."

"I didn't know that at the time. I had been sexually abused at a young age. For me, at that point in my life, sex was the one thing that I knew that I was good for. I made it work for me by dancing on poles rather than hustling johns on a street corner," Mary shrugged.

"Not every girl got the chance to get out. You did. I don't for a moment regret helping you," Chandler told her.

"And I love you for helping me get out. Because of you, I've been able to help other girls who wanted to get out. I call that a win-win," Mary smiled again.

"Yes," he said. "Yes, it is."

~ ~ ~

Ogden Spears was tall and muscular. He had light brown hair that was thinning, thick busy eyebrows, and a perpetual frown on his face nearly all the time. He was sitting in his trailer on a construction site reading the Indianapolis Star. He paid particular attention to a short article on the front page about a dead woman being discovered in the home of Arnie Grossman. That could be bad.

Grossman was one of his prime bankrollers for the number of civic center's being raised around town to help at risk teens to keep them out of gangs. If

Grossman was found guilty, it would mean that he would have to shut down all of his sites until he could find other financing. It really was going to be a bitch of a day.

~ ~ ~

Chandler had used a city directory to locate Sarah Luxor. It was mid-afternoon and he felt like he was trying to swim through quicksand. Arnie was scared shitless that he was going to go to jail for murder. Chandler had to make sure that didn't happen because he knew that Arnie had been set up. Somebody had built a nice neat frame for Arnie. Chandler had to figure out who?

He knocked on Sarah Luxor's door. He was surprised when she answered it herself, given the size of the house he had expected a butler or maid to answer. For the lady herself to answer, that had surprised him.

Sarah Luxor was around five foot five, slender without being skinny, curves and generous ones in all the right places. She had the face of a fashion model with high cheekbones and wide set eyes. Her dark hair cascaded down over her bare shoulders. Her lips were full and inviting as she beckoned him in. She was wearing a black tube top over short teal workout shorts. Her feet were bare and her nails and toes were painted the same shade as her shorts. "Can I help you?" she asked.

"Sarah Luxor? My name is Chandler and I need to talk to you," he replied.

"Well come in then," Sarah smiled invitingly. Chandler knew that he would have to watch himself with this one. He entered, closing the door behind him and followed her to an interior room, enjoying the show that she put into her hips as she walked. Chandler knew that was entirely for his benefit. She took a seat in a straight-backed chair on one side of a wide coffee table, Chandler took the seat across from her.

"What can I do for you?" Sarah asked.

"I want to ask you about last night, and the celebration you were having with Arnie Grossman," Chandler said.

"Ah, poor Arnie. He was getting sloppy drunk there towards the end. A couple of the guys had to carry him out and put him into a cab," Sarah smiled at the memory.

"Did anybody go home with him?"

"No, he was alone, at least when Ogden and John half-carried him out to the taxi. Arnie could barely keep his eyes open."

"Ogden being...?" He let it hang there even though he knew the answer.

"Ogden Spears, the contractor. John was John Irwin," Sarah shook her head as if Chandler was totally ignorant.

"Was Arnie showing particular attention to anyone in particular last night?"

"There was a girl, a little hot tamale who oozed sexuality hanging onto him towards the end. But she was still there after he left. What's this all about, anyway?"

"It appears somebody drugged Arnie last night and he woke up to find a dead woman in his house. He's being considered a 'person of interest' in her death."

"My God! Are you serious? Arnie Grossman

wouldn't hurt a fly. He's actually a very sensitive person," Sarah shook her head. That her assessment matched his was something Chandler didn't offer to tell her. Instead, he thanked her for her time and made a hasty exit, thinking at the time that she was a fine one to talk about another woman 'oozing' sexuality.

~ ~ ~

Mary Norman wore a tight-fitting blue pantsuit. The sandals that she wore were cork wedges that lifted her legs and made her butt look spectacular. She climbed out of her late model Ford Focus at Ogden Spears' main construction trailer.

It looked like any other construction site, with ten feet high chain link fence surrounding the site, a large gate that currently stood open so workers could pass in and out as needed, or supplies could be brought in. Mary followed the crushed stone drive to where the office trailer sat. Wooden steps led up to the door. She could hear a few catcalls from some of the workers as she walked. It didn't really bother her, as she had heard it all before when she was dancing.

Mary knocked on the door before opening it and stepping inside the trailer. Inside, she removed her sunglasses and hooked one of the temples on the edge of her purse. She could see a man that she was fairly certain was Ogden Spears through a sliding glass window in a wall that separated the office from the rest of the trailer. So far, the contractor hadn't noticed her, but she was certainly about to change that.

Mary walked to the open door that led into the office and stepped inside. "Mr. Spears? My name is Mary Norman and I'm working for Arnie Grossman's lawyer," she explained.

"How is Arnie doing?" Spears looked tired. Large bags hung under his eyes.

"As well as can be expected under the circumstances. I need to ask you about the celebration last night. How many clubs did you guys party at?" Mary asked.

"We stayed pretty much at Land Sharks. Arnie was okay early, but by eleven or so, he had turned into a sloppy drunk. He could barely stand and he was hitting hard of some little mamacita that had sex oozing out of her pores. She was packed tight into her pants and shirt and was showing a lot of cleavage. John Irwin and I called a taxi for Arnie and took him out and sent him home. That was the last I saw of him," Spears shrugged.

"What about the girl, the mamacita as you called her?" Mary asked.

"What about her?" Spears asked.

"Did she stay at the club or leave shortly after Arnie?"

"I really don't know. She wasn't part of our group, so I really didn't pay attention," Spears shrugged.

"If you think of anything else, please give me a call," Mary said, handing him a business card before standing and walking out. She knew that Spears was watching her so she made sure her hips were in full sway.

Mary returned to her car. She fastened her seatbelt and then started the engine. Something was bothering her, but she just couldn't say what it was at first. She would have to think on it a bit.

~ ~ ~

Johnny Quick paid no attention to the stripper on

stage. He was concentrating on a black gentleman sitting on the far side of the stage. His name was Travon Blake. Blake was the head of a local gang calling themselves the Mutants. Quick had seen his type many times before up in Detroit.

Johnny took a pull on his beer as he watched a couple of guys walk in and move towards Blake. Johnny watched as the first one leaned over and whispered in Blake's ear. Blake stood and followed the two men out the door. Johnny followed suit, glad that he had decided not to run a tab.

He followed the three men out into the parking lot and watched as they all climbed in to a dark blue Hummer. Johnny headed for his Chrysler Crossfire and followed them out into traffic.

~ ~ ~

Chandler arrived at the home of Melody Williams. It was a nice little two-story cottage with a stone walkway that led to the front door. It reminded him of a Tudor mansion he had seen once working undercover. There was a knocker and a bell on the door. Chandler opted for bell, figuring it would be the quickest to draw a response.

A young woman with red hair answered the door. She had a smattering of freckles across her nose and cheeks. Her hair was pulled back in a ponytail. She was wearing a tank top and shorts that showed off nice long legs. Chandler groaned inside. He was having a tough time battling against his libido. "Well, hello," Melody Williams smiled at him.

Chapter Five

"Miss Williams, I presume?" Chandler asked.

"Yes indeed," she smiled back.

"My name is Phillip Chandler. I'm working for Arnie Grossman."

"Wow, is he okay?"

"Why do you ask?"

"He was pretty loaded last night."

"Have you seen the news this morning?" Chandler asked.

"I haven't even turned on the television this morning," Melody shook her head.

"A woman was found dead in Mr. Grossman's house early this morning."

"How awful! Is Arnie okay?"

"He's as well as he can be, given the circumstances. Would you care to answer some questions for me?"

"Sure, I guess so. Come on in," Melody Williams stepped aside and beckoned for him to enter.

"Thank you," Chandler told her as he stepped inside and let the door close behind him. Melody turned and headed deeper into the house. Chandler followed, enjoying her hip-action as he walked. He knew that he should feel some small degree of guilt about that, but he was after all, only human. And male.

"Would you like some coffee?" she asked after directing him to a chair in the living room.

"Coffee would be good," Chandler smiled, giving her

one of his best. Gathering information was the bulk of his job. Looking around at the stylishly decorated room, Chandler knew that Miss Williams was not hurting for money.

A few moments later and Melody Williams reappeared carrying two coffee cups. She was barefoot and Chandler was very aware of her long legs and the way that the tube-top seemed to get smaller as she put a mug of coffee down on the table and took a seat opposite of him, folding her legs under her as she sat. Chandler took a sip of his coffee, it was pretty hot. He sat the mug down on a coaster on the coffee table that separated them. Melody Williams looked at him expectantly, hiding a smile behind her cup.

"Talk to me about last night please," Chandler said. It wasn't a question, more of a command.

"Arnie had just closed a deal for funding the remaining construction of the five community centers in at risk neighborhoods. Most of those in our party are on the board of Phoenix Rehabilitations, which is the foundation that Arnie created to try and help keep kids out of trouble," Melody explained.

"Do you know where he got the funding?" Chandler asked.

"Why do you ask?"

"Well, you said yourself; you're on the board of directors. It seems like something that you would know."

"Well, I don't. Arnie didn't say," Melody frowned. She seemed to be getting somewhat evasive.

"Didn't anyone ask?"

"Mr. Chandler, I think that it's past time that you

leave," Melody said harshly. Her face no longer looked pretty; her skin seemed to tighten over her cheekbones, giving her a somewhat gaunt look.

"I'll leave for now, Ms. Williams, but this isn't the end of this conversation. We will be talking again," Chandler told her as he stood. "I know the way out." He headed for the front door, stepping outside and closing it and heading for his SUV. That had certainly been an interesting interview. Melody Williams was hiding something. Chandler wanted to know what.

~ ~ ~

Mary looked at the list of names. John Irwin, Harold Gore, and Fabian Morales. John Irwin was the most prominent man on the list. He did almost as much for the community as Arnie Grossman. She would save him for last. So, Gore or Morales? Which one should she try next? Mentally she flipped a coin. Gore was the closest. She started her car, and slipped out into the Saturday traffic.

~ ~ ~

Harold Gore rarely worked on the weekends. Once the markets closed, his week was over until the following Monday. Gore was a portly man in his mid-fifties with a ruddy complexion and a nose filled with broken veins, testimony no doubt to his love of bourbon, which he tended to ingest in great quantities. He still had a full head of silver gray hair and bushy white brows that loomed over his eyes like furry caterpillars.

He was dressed in long khaki shorts and a green aloha shirt covered with plants and multi-colored birds. He had on white socks and had on a pair of Nike shower sandals. "Can I help you?" he asked Mary when he opened the door.

"Mister Gore, I'm an investigator working on behalf of Arnold Grossman. I was hoping that you could answer some questions about the celebration last night?"

"Why does Arnie need an investigator?" Gore asked, looking confused.

"I take it you haven't seen the news or read the newspaper?" Mary asked him.

"I rarely get to that before the afternoon," Gore waved a hand dismissively.

"Mister Grossman woke up this morning and found the body of a dead woman in his living room. He was taken in and questioned as a person of interest by the police. His attorney hired my partner's firm to look into the case," Mary explained.

"Good Lord! Poor Arnie. He did seem to be well into his cups last night when John and Ogden took him out of the club and put him in the taxi. I sincerely doubt that he could have killed anyone. He could barely stand under his own power," Gore supplied.

"Was there anyone who seemed to take a special interest in him at the bar?"

"There was one young lady, but she was not with him when he left."

"Can you describe her for me? Really, any information at all will be helpful."

"I didn't catch her name, but she was young, beautiful and obviously of a Hispanic background. She was quite a dish if you get my drift."

"I do indeed. Do you remember when she left?"

"I saw her going out the door about half an hour after Arnie was sent home to sleep it off."

"Did you see her again that night?"

"No, and I left shortly after she did."

"Thank you for your time, Mr. Gore. This was indeed helpful," Mary told him as she stood. Gore stood as well and escorted her back to the door. Once outside, Mary returned to her car. She took a moment to write down notes about the interview, which she would expand on later when she played the digital recording back of the interview. Then she started her car and backed out of the driveway to go see Fabian Morales.

~ ~ ~

Gwen Franks was a rather mousey young woman with a buttoned-down blouse, mousey brown hair, dark-rimmed glasses, and a pair of high-waisted slacks and two inch heels. A single gold chain hung around her neck. She was very out of place compared to the other women that had been in the party. "Miss Franks?" Chandler asked, trying to ascertain that he was indeed at the right place.

"Yes, and who might you be?" She asked, peering at him over the tops of her glasses, which Chandler noticed had a thin chain hanging from the earpieces to secure them.

"My name is Phillip Chandler. I'm an investigator working for Arnie Grossman," he identified himself.

"Why would Arnie need an investigator?" she looked like she didn't believe him. Chandler handed her one of his business card along with a photocopy of his license. Gwen Franks took them and studied them before handing them back.

"Arnie woke up with a dead woman in his house this morning. She was spotted with him last night at the club in Broad Ripple where you were all celebrating," Chandler explained.

"Oh my God!" one hand went to her mouth.

"I need you to tell me about last night."

"Tell me what you want to know," Gwen replied.

~ ~ ~

Johnny Quick stayed on Travon Blake. Blake was known to move a lot of product in Broad Ripple, but even Quick knew that he wasn't the local kingpin. Travon Blake worked for somebody. Johnny wanted to know who. He followed Blake back towards the downtown.

Blake swung off onto 10th street, heading east. He finally stopped in front of a two-story house that set back off the sidewalk. Quick pulled to the curb about half a block back and shut off his engine. He watched as Blake and the two men marched up onto the porch. One of the men knocked and the door opened and they went inside.

Johnny stepped out of his car. In this neighborhood, he wouldn't even be noticed. He walked down the sidewalk past the house, making note of the house number. He stepped inside a corner store and looked around for a few moments before heading back towards his car carrying a paper bag holding a magazine and a couple of donuts. He also had a coffee in his hand. Just another guy from the neighborhood.

Johnny Quick climbed back into his car, sipping from the cup of coffee. He pulled a donut out of the bag and took a bite. It tasted good. He washed it down with a drink of coffee. Nobody came out of the house. He figured that this might well turn out to be a long day.

~ ~ ~

"What exactly was your role with Mr. Grossman?" Chandler asked.

"I'm an accountant," Gwen said.

"So, you handled the cash for the community centers?"

"I did."

"Where did the money come from?"

"What do you mean?"

"Where did the money to fund the civic center's come from?"

"I'm afraid that is privileged information," Gwen Franks shook her head.

"Meaning?" Chandler asked.

"I cannot tell you. It's bound in client privilege," Gwen replied.

"What if Arnie gives you permission to talk to me?" Chandler asked.

"Then I could talk to you," she admitted.

"Let me make a call then," Chandler told her. He pulled out his phone and dialed Arnie Grossman's number.

~ ~ ~

Mary Norman frowned at the recording device in her hand. She had played back the early interviews, and she really had not liked what she had heard. She hoped that her interview with Fabian Morales would give her more detail about what had happened with Arnie Grossman before he had left the club.

She put her car in gear and headed for the address on

43

the west side that she had for Morales. She parked her car outside of the gated house in Fishers. Mary walked up to the button on the intercom in the driveway. She pressed the call button.

"Hello?" asked a tinny voice through the intercom.

"My name is Mary Norman and I am here to see Mr. Morales," she said.

"Mr. Morales would like to know why?" the voice replied.

"It has to do with Arnie Grossman," she replied.

"One moment please," said a voice on the other end. Mary waited. She looked over the grounds that were visible through the wrought iron gate. The house looked almost like a Victorian mansion. Whoever Fabian Morales was, he had a ton of money at his disposal. Had he been one of Arnie Grossman's investors?

"You may drive up to the house," the intercom crackled at her and the gates began to creak open in their motor-driven guides. Mary walked back to her car and climbed inside, restarted the motor and drove through the opening. In her rearview mirror, she watched the gates roll closed behind her. It was a very unsettling feeling.

~ ~ ~

Gwen Franks handed Chandler his cell phone back, seemingly satisfied that he was indeed working for Arnie Grossman. "Please have a seat," Gwen said.

Chapter Six

Two hours later, Blake and the two men came out of the house and got back into their car and drove away. He debated on following them and decided to sit on the house. Blake had come here for a reason. Quick wanted to know why.

Johnny Quick frowned. He wasn't sure why he was doing this, other than Chandler had asked him to. He had to admit that he was at something of loose ends after walking away from the Detroit Mob scene. Chandler had worked out a deal with his old boss so that the old man wouldn't come after him as long as he never ever went back to Detroit again. That was something that Johnny was okay with. Detroit was too goddam cold in the winter. Usually Indy wasn't much better, but this year the winter had been fairly mild.

Of course, he still took the occasional overseas job if the money was right. But there hadn't been a lot of offers of late. Mercenary work needed active wars. Most were winding down. Which meant that now he was helping a private eye doing grunt work.

Chandler sipped at his cup of coffee as he studied Gwen Franks over the rim of the cup. After speaking to Arnie, she seemed much more relaxed. "So, tell, me, Miss Franks, where did the financial windfall come from?"

"Part of it came from Fabian Morales. The rest of it was from a different investor, a man named Luther

Brookshire. He is a local businessman. Mr. Morales had helped put together a small syndicate to help with the centers," Gwen explained.

"What can you tell me about Mr. Morales and Mr. Brookshire?"

"They were both investors in the community that is really all I know."

"Did they bear any ill will towards Arnie?"

"None that I know of."

"Thank you, Gwen. You may not realize it, but this actually does help," Chandler told her.

"I'm glad I could help," Gwen smiled at him. Chandler nodded and turned and walked out the front door.

~ ~ ~

Alejandro Cruz looked at the crime scene photos that had been taken in Arnie Grossman's house. The dead woman had been beautiful when alive, some of that carried over into the pictures of her in death. She had died too young. She was of Hispanic descent. He hated cases involving young people. They had too much to live for. He dropped the picture on his desk and reached for his coffee mug. He took a sip. Damn it had gone cold.

Bad enough that the case involved Arnie Grossman. The guy was a major moneyman. He was also a philanthropist who had done a lot for the city. Cruz hated high-profile cases like this. He hadn't bought Grossman's temporary amnesia bit. Then the results of the blood draw had come back showing a large amount of rohypnol in his blood stream. The guy was lucky that he had awakened at all.

The fact that Chandler was working for Grossman made things worse. The former Deputy U.S. Marshal turned private eye was a colossal pain in the ass. However, Chandler was damn good at finding the truth.

~ ~ ~

Mary felt a growing sense of unease as she approached the large house. Several men wearing dark suits and sunglasses stood at regular intervals around the mansion. One man stood out away from them and he appeared to be waiting on her. Mary parked her car on the circular drive and got out, locking the doors behind her. The lone man approached her.

"Miss Norman? I'm Luis Lopez. Mister Morales is awaiting you inside," the man said.

"Thank you for showing me in," Mary told him. She had put on her work face, the same one that she used back in her days as a dancer.

Mary followed him inside, divorcing herself from her surroundings, using all the tricks she had learned on stage to mask what she was feeling inside. She didn't know what it was, but something about Fabian Morales frightened her. As much as she hated it, she found herself wishing that Chandler was with her to keep her safe. It was a feeling that she hated having, but she also knew that it was part of what had drawn her to Chandler to begin with. He had a presence that was both protective and calming. For the first time since they had faced down The Circle[2], Mary Norman was afraid.

---

[2]

Circle City Shakedown

The inside of the house was amazing. Dark paneling covered the walls. The carpet was thick and plush. Lopez led her to a thick walnut door. He paused outside to knock twice, and then he opened the door and ushered Mary inside. Mary hadn't been sure what to expect but then she saw that Fabian Morales looked like Andy Garcia. She relaxed a little.

"Mr. Morales?" she asked.

"Yes. And you are?" he let it linger in the air between them.

"My name is Mary Norman. I am working for Arnie Grossman," Mary managed to reply.

"How is Arnie? He wasn't looking well last night when he left," Morales said, with a slight smirk.

"He had been drugged at the club. I was wondering if you had noticed anyone that had been hanging around him?" Mary asked.

"There was a young woman, I don't remember her name. She seemed to show a great deal of interest in Arnie."

"I understand that you had put a lot of money into the civic centers. Is that part of what the celebration last night was about?" Mary asked, looking him in the eye. Morales looked down to the left before answering.

"I had contributed some of his funding. Like our dear Arnie, I want to help keep the inner-city youth out of gangs. I felt that the civic centers were the best way to accomplish that," Morales shrugged.

"Were there other donors?"

"I'm sure there were. Arnie would know more about them than I would. I just wrote a few checks," Morales said smoothly. It was almost too smooth, like greased silk thread.

"I'll make sure to ask him about that then. Did you notice anyone paying particular attention to Mr. Grossman last night?" Mary was getting a bad vibe off of Morales and she wanted to get away from him as quickly as possible.

"There was a young woman hanging all over him at the club, but he left without her."

"Thank you for your time, Mr. Morales. I really need to run. There are some other people I need to talk to."

"Are you sure you have to rush off? I was hoping you might stay for a drink," Morales smiled at her.

"No, I really need to run," Mary said, standing and slinging her bag over her shoulder. Her hand slipped inside to wrap around the butt of her .38 Special. She turned and headed for the door, fighting the urge to break into a run. Once she was outside the house, she was able to slow down her breathing. Mary walked quickly to her car, pulling out the keys and unlocking it and slipping inside. She activated the electronic locks immediately. Putting the keys in the ignition, she started the engine before buckling her seatbelt. Then she put the car in gear and headed for the gate. Thankfully it was open and she was able to drive right on out and onto the street. Mary drove to a nearby strip mall and then called Chandler.

~ ~ ~

Chandler was on his way to the J.D. Marriott downtown when his cell phone rang. Sampson had put Arnie in a room at the hotel since his house was still considered a crime scene.

"Mary, how is it going?" Chandler asked.

"I think we need to take a closer look at Fabian Morales," Mary said breathlessly.

"Did you get something out of him?" Chandler asked, suddenly alert.

"Just a very bad feeling. I wouldn't be surprised if he wasn't the one that planted the dead girl in Arnie's house," Mary replied.

"I've learned to trust your feelings. Where are you now?" Mary gave him her location.

"Head back to the office. I'll meet you there," Chandler told her. He decided that he could talk to Arnie later. Mary needed him.

~ ~ ~

Arnie Grossman took a drink of the Jim Beam bourbon. How had all this happened? He was a murder suspect, but he had no memory of killing anyone. He remembered Tiffany, but not much else. He had really liked her. She had hung on his every word. She had seemed to really understand him when he had expounded on his theories on social engineering. Now she was gone. He could still see her lying on his floor, an expanding pool of blood beneath her head, her hair spread in the blood sticking to the vinyl floor.

Arnie slugged back the drink. All he had wanted to do was help the inner- city children. Who had gone to all of this trouble to frame him for a murder that he hadn't committed? Hopefully Chandler would be able to find an answer to that.

~ ~ ~

Johnny Quick had continued to sit on the house on 10th street. Finally, an older black man emerged from the house. When he reached the sidewalk, he turned and headed towards the store that Quick had visited earlier. He decided that it might be time to pay the store a second visit.

Johnny climbed out of his car and headed down the street towards the store. The sun was hot overhead in the springtime sky. He wanted to know who the old man was. Johnny had a feeling that it would be important.

~ ~ ~

Mary was shaking when Chandler pulled into the parking space beside her. He shut off his engine and stepped out, opening her door. Mary stepped out and Chandler folded her into his arms. He let her feel his strength as she melted against him. He had never seen her this frightened. It made him angry deep inside. Finally, she stopped sobbing and pushed him away, reaching back into her car for a Kleenex. Mary blew her nose and then used a second tissue to clean up her face.

"Better now?" Chandler asked her.

"Somewhat. I have a bad feeling about Fabian Morales. He made me feel like a victim. I didn't like that," Mary said softly.

"I don't like anyone making you feel like that," Chandler told her.

"It pisses me off," Mary said. Chandler could hear the anger in her voice.

"Let's head inside and we can talk about it," Chandler told her.

"Yes, I've got a lot to tell you."

"Me too," Chandler replied.

~ ~ ~

Alejandro Cruz pulled up in front of the Fishers home of John Irwin, the owner of the Indianapolis

Stallions. Irwin was probably the biggest name attached to the Arnie Grossman party that had been at the celebration. That was why Cruz had decided to talk to him first, hopefully before Chandler got to him. For once, Cruz wanted to be a few steps ahead of the former Deputy Marshal.

Cruz was surprised when an honest-to-God butler answered the front door. The man was in full livery complete with black tails. The man had a fringe of short gray hair forming a half circle around his shiny bald pate. His nose was hawkish and his eyes were of a similar gray color as his hair.

"Mister Irwin is expecting you, Sir," the butler said. Cruz nodded and followed the man inside. After the door was shut behind them he led Cruz through an opulent mansion. They reached a flight of wide stairs that led up to a second floor. Cruz counted thirty-six from the floor to the second floor. They traveled down a hallway and stopped before two thick oaken doors. The butler knocked and Cruz heard a voice yell to come in. The Butler opened the door and ushered him inside. "Detective Cruz, Sir," the man introduced him.

John Irwin was a tall man, once he had been an impressive athlete, but the years had taken their toll on him. He had a slight bend to his back, and his shoulders were hunched slightly. It was no secret that he had been battling an addiction to painkillers due to chronic pain. He had been arrested more than once for substance abuse, because of it. "It's a pleasure to meet you, Detective Cruz."

"And you as well, Sir. Though I am afraid that I wish that the circumstances were better," Cruz replied, shaking hands.

"I wish the same thing, believe me. I don't for a minute believe that Arnie killed that young woman," Irwin told him.

"Can you tell me why you believe that?" Cruz asked.

"Arnie was not a guy that would get physical with anyone, let alone a woman. Arnie was a coward at the best of times when it came to brawling. He hates confrontation," Irwin explained.

"Talk to me about the girl that was hitting on him," Cruz directed.

"She was a pill. She was pure sex wrapped up in too tight pants and a low-cut top that she was damn near spilling out of. She didn't give me the time of day, even though she knew who I was. She was totally focused on Arnie. So, I figured what the hell and got out of the way. I helped Ogden Spears put Arnie in a cab. I left soon after that," Irwin explained.

Chapter Seven

"**A**re you feeling better now?" Chandler asked as he watched her sip at the tumbler of Jim Beam on ice.

She was sitting in the client chair on the opposite side of the desk from him. He had figured that a couple of fingers of bourbon would calm her nerves.

"As much as I can be, I guess," Mary replied, taking in a deep breath and letting it out slowly.

"Are you ready to talk to me about it?"

"I don't know if I'll ever be ready to talk about it. But I will talk to you about it."

"So, where do you want to start?"

Mary took another sip of Jim Beam. "I started with Ogden Spears first. He gave me pretty much the same story. They had all gone to Land Sharks to celebrate. Arnie got sloppy really fast, quicker than he should have. There was this young Hispanic gal named Tiffany that kept hitting on him. But he left ahead of her."

"That matches pretty close to what I learned from the ladies I interviewed," Chandler nodded. Mary took another sip and closed her eyes. Chandler could feel the tension building inside her again.

"Harold Gore gave me pretty much the same story. He also commented about the young Hispanic woman that was all over Arnie Grossman. He was very descriptive about her sexual impulses where Arnie was concerned. He also stated that she left at least an hour after Arnie was sent home," Mary explained.

"That certainly agrees with the timeline I was able to get as well," Chandler nodded. Mary gulped down the rest of the bourbon. Chandler poured her some more.

"Are you trying to get me drunk?" Mary asked.

"I might be, if it will make sure that I get lucky later."

"You'll always get lucky with me, Chandler."

"I know. Now what was it about Morales that freaked you out so much?"

"I'm not exactly sure. I think it might have been the opulence of his home. He had gates across his driveway. When I entered, and saw the gates closing behind me, it gave me the feeling that I might not ever get out."

"Why do you think that is?"

"I think that as I watched the gates close, I became aware that I was no longer in control. Morales had taken the control away from me. It made me feel as helpless as when the Circle was after me," Mary explained.

"Interesting. Was there anything else?" Chandler asked.

"Part of it was the way that he looked at me. Like I was nothing more than a meaningless dish at a buffet. He wasn't unsettled, it was as if he were totally in control. He Looked at me as if I were a piece of meat, even as he admitted that he had put a great deal of funding into Arnie's project." Mary shivered at the memory and took another gulp from her glass.

"Okay, it sounds like he might be someone we want to look into a little more. See what you can find about him on the databases. Any more personal contact will come from me. I don't like seeing you frightened."

"I don't like being frightened. But Fabian Morales frightened me, Phillip."

"I'll look forward to meeting him in person," Chandler told her. The smile on his face would have frightened most people. Mary threw her arms around him and hugged him tightly. Chandler hugged her back.

"John Irwin is the last of the celebrants that we have to interview about last night. I think he can wait until tomorrow," Chandler said.

"Can you take me home now?" Mary asked quietly.

"I can. You could use a nap," Chandler said.

"Yes, I could," Mary nodded before tossing back the rest of her drink. Chandler capped the bottle and put it back in his desk drawer. He helped Mary up and let her lean on him on the way out to the Bronco. Chandler buckled her in and drove to the home they shared in Beach Grove. Mary was snoring softly in the passenger seat. He parked in the garage and then carried her to the bed that they shared. He pulled down the covers, removed her shoes and tucked her in. Then he went back to the kitchen and fired up his laptop. There were several things that he wanted to check. Simba rubbed against his legs. Chandler knelt down and scratched the cat behind the ears and rubbed his back and belly. Simba headed for the bedroom where Chandler knew that he would leap up onto the bed and snuggle close to Mary and go to sleep.

~ ~ ~

Johnny Quick headed for The Red Garter. He knew a couple of guys that might be willing to tell him who lived in that house on 10th street. They usually hung out at the Garter.

The doorman let Johnny in without bothering to charge him the cover. He knew Johnny and Johnny knew him. He took a seat and ordered a beer. He kept his eyes on the stage as a slender redhead danced onto the stage in accompaniment of "Born to be Wild" on the jukebox. She was a pleasant enough distraction as he looked for familiar faces in the crowd. He moved to the stage and stuffed a five in her G-string before heading back to his table. She would come around and he could ask her some questions.

Johnny had a way with women, even strippers. They liked him. It didn't hurt that he tipped well, either. This was stuff Chandler would probably have handled himself before he got involved with Mary Norman, but Chandler was now a one-woman-man. Johnny never would be. No, having a woman would interfere with his autonomy, and that was something that Johnny would never give up. He never let anyone in enough to hurt him. That had happened once when he was a young man. Afterwards he had vowed it would never happen again.

Chandler was his friend, but it was not a conventional type friendship. Quick and Chandler both understood that. Mary Norman came close to understanding it, though it sometimes still mystified her. Quick smiled. Mary was one of a kind, and Chandler was lucky to have found her. Or, she was lucky to have found him. Johnny shook his head as he took a pull at his beer.

Life was complicated. The dancer finished her number and gathered up ones that had fallen on stage as the deejay announced the next girl. Quick took another drink of his beer. She would be out soon enough.

~ ~ ~

Alejandro Cruz drove back to the Metro station, satisfied about his talk with John Irwin. He had no doubt that the man had told him to the truth. But there were other witnesses to interview as well. Cruz was wary about interviewing the city's royalty. They lived in a different world. The Circle had proved that.[3]

This was not going to be an easy case. The fact that power players and big money were involved made it more complicated than Cruz liked. But there was nothing he could do about that

~ ~ ~

Chandler shut down the laptop. He changed into running clothes and grabbed his .22 and put it in the pocket of his hoodie. He set the alarms before leaving and hit the street. Running cleared his mind. He knew all the things about endorphins released by exercise. They were supposed to give a high similar to the one released by sex. Personally, Chandler felt that was bullshit. Sex was way better. Still, running allowed him an escape from everything.

It was a way of letting go of everything for the time of the run. It cleared his head and allowed him to lose himself in the rhythm of his stride. He ran for two miles, and then turned and ran back to the house. He slowed to a walk about a block away to let his heart start slowing down.

---

[3]

Circle City Shakedown

Who had killed the girl and left her in Arnie Grossman's house? That was the question of the day. Was it a warning? Or was it something else entirely? It was a puzzle to be sure. One that he had to put together. When he solved the puzzle, he would know who was behind the frame.

Still, he had to wonder who it was that wanted to frame Arnie? It was a question that needed answering. Who would want to stop the construction of the civic centers? Chandler pulled out a toothpick, and stuck it into his mouth, rolling it to a corner and chewing on it.

Chewing on the toothpick helped him think. It was a habit that Mary was trying to break him of, but she had not managed to succeed, at least not so far. To Chandler, it was a lot better than smoking.

Chandler walked the last half a block to the home that he shared now with Mary. He heard the engine of a car rev up after he had passed it. Chandler spun, dropping into a crouch, the .22 automatic filling his hand. The car leaped towards him. Chandler fired. The windshield spider-webbed and the car swung away from the curb. Chandler emptied the .22 into the windows. Shattered glass fell to the pavement before the car swerved around a corner a block away.

Chandler watched it go, wondering who was inside the car. He would find out. One way or another. He upped the safety on the .22 and dialed 9-1-1. He had fired a gun and the police would want to know why. He walked to the front porch and took a seat in one of the two the plastic chairs that decorated it. He would wait for the police there so that he wouldn't disturb Mary's rest.

~ ~ ~

It took about half an hour for the uniform to take the report. They didn't try to take the little .22 since there wasn't a body attached to it. At least not yet. Still, the night was young. Chandler unlocked the door and slipped inside. He made his way to the bathroom and stripped down, leaving the pistol on the toilet tank beside his towel. The curtain slid back and Mary stepped in beside him. "Hey Sailor, do you come here often," she asked seductively.

"If you're here, every chance I get," Chandler replied as he gathered her in his arms and pulled her towards him, kissing her mouth hard. Her seeking hands found him.

"Yes, and you're hard to miss," Mary smiled at him. Chandler lifted her up and she slid down onto him. For the next fifteen minutes, getting clean was the last thing on their minds.

~ ~ ~

"You haven't been in much lately," Laurie said as she took a seat at Johnny Quick's table. Laurie was the stripper that he had tipped so well.

"I've been busy. Security jobs," Johnny shrugged.

"So, to what do I owe the pleasure of your company, tonight?" she asked, her eyes sparkling.

"I'm looking for a couple of guys that hang out around here. Goose and Pinta. They been in tonight?" Johnny asked.

"Not yet, but they should be soon. Goose has a thing for Melody and she comes on at 8 o'clock. I get off at ten," Laurie told him.

"I need to talk to Goose about a house on East

Tenth Street, then how about we catch a late dinner over at St. Elmo's?" Johnny asked her.

"I'd like that," Laurie told him. Johnny slipped her a twenty.

"Let me know when Goose shows," he told her.

"Will do," Laurie smiled, standing up to work the room. Johnny watched her go. Laurie was a good kid. He liked her, but she liked her life too much to change it for any man.

~ ~ ~

Arnie Grossman was pacing like a caged lion. He was afraid to even order room service. Somebody was trying to frame him for murder! Who could it be? And why? All he was trying to do was help the youth of this city! He wanted to keep them from joining gangs, help them educate themselves, help them makes something of themselves! But somebody didn't want that to happen? Who could have murdered that poor girl, Tiffany?

He had purchased a bottle of Jim Beam after leaving the police station. Sampson had been with him. Sampson had declined to stay with him after securing him in the room at the Marriott. Arnie stripped the plastic off of one of the glasses in the room. He added a couple of ice cubes before pouring in two fingers of bourbon.

It burned going down, but it was smooth enough that he barely noticed. Getting drunk again probably wasn't the smartest idea that he had, but it would at the very least allow him to sleep the night through. Tiffany and been a lot of fun, even if she was just there for a chance to hang with a millionaire. He would have liked to have gotten to know her better, and certainly more intimately. She had inferred that she would not be averse to that. But somebody had killed her. Murdered her before it could happen. And they had left her dead body in his house. Arnie tossed back the drink and poured himself another one.

Chapter Eight

Chandler and Mary walked out of St. Elmo's hand in hand. The air was cool, down in the fifties, unusual for this late in May. Mary leaned against Chandler's left shoulder. "This has been a nice evening, much better than the day we had," she told him.

"Yes, it has. It might get even better." Chandler leaned down and kissed the top of her head.

"I'm not sure how," Mary looked up at him.

"We're off to Land Sharks now," Chandler told her as they approached where he had parked the Bronco.

"Somehow I get the feeling it's not just for an evening of dancing and fun?"

"You would be right. We've got this case to work. Maybe some of the same people will be there tonight that were there last night. We need to find out more about the dead girl and what her interest was in Arnie Grossman," Chandler unlocked the Bronco and held the door open for Mary. She climbed inside, waiting to speak until he had gone around the car and climbed inside.

"Do you find that interest to be odd?" Mary asked.

"In some respects, I do. The young woman was less than half Arnie's age, and by all accounts vivacious and exuding a strong amount of sensuality and sexual desire. Unless she had Daddy issues, yes, I do find her interest in him out of the norm." Chandler turned on the engine and put the SUV in gear, checking the mirrors before signaling and then pulling out into traffic.

"Young women like to date older men that they fantasize will do anything for them. I saw a lot of that in my former life," Mary pointed out.

"The Sugar Daddy syndrome," Chandler offered.

"Or something very similar," Mary agreed.

"Why do you think that she chose Arnie to hit on?"

"There could be many reasons for it. He has celebrity status, he's been in the news a lot here lately. Maybe she felt that she would appeal to him? According to the others in the party, she seemed to. At least until Arnie got so sloppy drunk that he had to be sent home."

"Except that we now know that his drinks were being spiked with rohypnol, which is considered to be a date rape drug. Could Tiffany have been spiking his drink? Or someone else?" Chandler asked.

"I'm not sure there would be any way to know that for sure, since she's dead and we can't ask her," Mary replied.

"Which is why we are heading to the club tonight. Arnie's party would have drawn attention, even in Broad Ripple," Chandler explained.

"You believe that somebody might have seen whoever spiked Arnie's drink," Mary eyed him.

"I do. I also believe that there might be some of the dead woman's friends there as well. They might be able to answer questions about her and her intentions towards Arnie Grossman. Was it her idea, or was he suggested to her as a man that she might do well to meet?"

"I suspect that is my job, to find that out?"

"I think any of her friends might open up about things like that more for you than they would for me," Chandler shrugged.

"I suspect you'd be right in that. Of course, you'll be questioning men who might have observed anything?" Mary asked.

"That is my plan, yes," Chandler smiled. He pulled into the parking lot of Land Sharks. Traffic had been light during the 23-minute drive.

"Well, then park this beast and let's get inside so we can get to work. One night soon, however, I expect to be taken out on a date that isn't work related," Mary told him archly.

"You wish is my command my love," Chandler grinned at her.

"If only," Mary rolled her eyes, trying but not succeeding in hiding her grin.

~ ~ ~

Johnny Quick was on his third bottle of beer when Lauren flashed him the high sign that Goose and Pinta had arrived. They were running late and had missed Melody's first set of dancing. Johnny observed them both from across the room as they took seats along the stage. It was a Saturday Night and the Red Garter was doing a booming business. They had girls working all four stages and Melody was next up for the main stage.

Johnny picked up his beer and made his way to the stage. He dropped into a vacant seat next to Goose. Goose was focused on Melody so he didn't really even notice that Johnny Quick had sat down next to him. Pinta was on the other side, trying to take in the whole club and all of the dancers at once. Johnny leaned over and nudged Goose.

"Goose. We need to talk," Johnny whispered into his ear.

"Who the fuck are you?" Goose demanded as he jerked around to look at Quick.

"Goose, I'm somebody you don't want to get on the bad side of," Johnny told him, flashing a white-toothed smile.

"Listen, Asshole, I don't give a fuck who you think you are, but nobody tells me I have to talk to them," Goose snarled.

"I disagree," Johnny told him as he poked the muzzle of a gun into Goose's gut. "You talk or you die. It is just that simple," Johnny said.

"What the hell do you want to know?" Goose asked, scared shitless now.

"I want to know the name of an old man that lives on East 10th Street. A guy that gets regular visits from local gang bangers."

"You mean Luther Donlley," Goose sighed.

"Luther Donlley. Tell me more," Quick whispered.

"Luther runs the black gangs around town for Fabian Morales. Morales is big in local organized crime," Goose sighed.

"The Fuzz know that?" Quick asked.

"No reason why they shouldn't, though Morales likes to keep his hands clean and has Luther run things at the street level," Goose spoke softly. Pinta hadn't even noticed his friend's predicament. His eyes were glued to the dancer on stage.

"Tell me more about Luther. He the kind of guy that would target a man and then kill a girl and dump her body in his house to frame him?"

"Yeah, Luther be capable of doing something like that. Luther's a hard man and he don't take no shit from nobody. Even Morales walks soft around him, and Luther is his employee!"

"You best keep this conversation to yourself, Goose. You go talking about it, you're not going to live too long. If I don't get you, Luther or one of his boys might well take you out," Quick told him.

"Yes, Sir," Goose whimpered, tears filling his eyes.

"Man up, Goose. Man-up or get out of town and get away from the game. You ain't near tough enough for it," Johnny patted his shoulder, stood up and walked back to his original table. Lauren appeared with two more beers in hand, and she was dressed in street clothes, which tonight meant a pair of dark slacks, stiletto heels, and a white button down shirt with a short black jacket. Her face was stripped clean of stage make-up and she wore a pale pink shade of lipstick.

"You get your business taken care of?" she asked, handing him one beer.

"I did. Let's sit for a few and finish these, we can go get a bite afterwards. I promised you someplace nice," Quick told her.

"Yes, you did."

"How about The Eagle? I've heard good things about the food," Lauren told him.

"You got it," Quick told her as he drained his beer in three swallows. Lauren finished hers almost as quickly. They walked out of the Red Garter hand in hand.

~ ~ ~

Fabian Morales sat in his study. He was enough of an

old-fashioned Spaniard that he preferred to have a study than a so-called 'man-cave'. Morales was a reader. He studied history. He was well educated and known as a man of impeccable manners and taste. Few people knew that he was also the head of a vast criminal organization that stretched from the United States into Mexico. Morales worked hard to keep his public face and his private face separate.

Being seen as a well-known businessman and entrepreneur was good for him. It distracted the authorities from his illegal dealings in the city. Luther took care of that for him. He smoked a cigar as he thought about his latest venture.

Investing in the community was a good thing. It elevated his profile as an entrepreneur, willing to help the city grow. What many didn't understand was that the civic centers were places that he could launder money through. He could also use them to recruit more teens to peddle narcotics for him. Grossman was a fool to think that he could stop that from happening.

Morales took a sip of his tequila. It ran smoothly over the salt on the rim of the shot glass that he had already twisted a slice of lime into. Before, he had not been allowed to join the Circle because of his race. Now, he was starting to rebuild the organization that had ostracized him.

~ ~ ~

Land Sharks was jumping as Chandler and Mary entered. Chandler had opted to leave his Colt at home tonight, going instead with a Ruger LC9S 9mm pistol in a pocket holster. He never went anywhere unarmed. A holdover from his days as a Deputy U.S. Marshal.

Once they were inside, Chandler bought them drinks, a beer for him and wine for her. There were a couple of gals up on stage singing to the Spice Girls on the karaoke machine. Chandler took out a toothpick and stripped off the cellophane before sticking it into the corner of his mouth. He took a sip of his beer. Killian's Red, his favorite.

Mary had drifted off to mingle with some of the female regulars. Chandler knew that she could take care of herself. She had proven that in the past. Chandler spotted a group of about five guys huddled around a television set mounted on the wall. They were watching the Cubs take on the Lions. So far, the Cubbies had the lead, but they had a batter up with no one on and a 3-2 count. Chandler joined the crowd. He was a Tiger's fan from way back.

Verlander was pitching and he easily struck the batter out to end the inning. "I don't believe the Cubs will be able to repeat," Chandler shook his head.

"Maybe, but it's still early in the season," offered a guy to his right.

"Yes, it is. You here last night?" Chandler asked him.

"Yeah, I was. Lot of well to do folks in here partying last night," the guy said.

"You got a name?" Chandler asked.

"Mark Franks," the guy introduced himself.

"Phil Chandler. So, there were some actual big wigs here last night?" Chandler asked.

"Oh, hell yeah. You should have been here! Arnie Grossman, the guy behind the civic centers, John Irwin that owns the Stallions, and a bunch of others," Franks explained.

"Wow, that is some bunch," Chandler nodded.

"It was. There was this really hot Hispanic Gal that was coming on to Grossman all night. She had the hots for him and if he hadn't got so drunk, he'd have taken her home and into bed," Franks said.

"So she didn't leave with him?" Chandler asked.

"Aw hell, no. She was really disappointed too. You could tell from the look on her face. But a couple of the guys that were with him took him out and put him in a cab home," Franks explained.

"Did you see her again after that?" Chandler asked.

"About half an hour after he left, she got a call and then headed out the door. She didn't look happy, but that might be because Grossman had shut her down before he was helped out of the place."

"What do you mean, he had shut her down?"

"Well he said something to her that appeared to piss her off right before his friends hustled him out. She looked pretty angry," Franks lifted his hands, indicating that his story had come to an end.

"That's quite a tale my friend," Chandler told him.

"Like I don't know that?" Franks grinned.

"You sure it is the truth?" Chandler asked.

"As God is my witness, Brother," Franks said.

"I believe you," Chandler said. He moved away. He still had a lot to think about. The Hispanic girl, Tiffany. She had appeared to target Arnie Grossman. Why was that? It was an interesting question. One that Chandler was bound and determined to find answers to!

Chapter Nine

"Pinta, we got us some trouble," Goose told his associate after he watched Johnny Quick and one of the dancers leave together.

"What kind of trouble?" Pinta was a thin wiry-looking guy with nervous eyes that were always darting around, trying to see everything at once.

"Some big black guy, told us to get out of town. He was askin' about Luther," Goose said as quietly as possible.

"Oh Jesus, that could be bad. Did you say anything?" Pinta's eyes widened and started moving more rapidly.

"Do you think I'm nuts? 'Course I didn't say nothing! I don't want to be killed. I think maybe we should put the word out about this guy looking for Luther. Luther gets wind of it, he'll take the big bastard out."

"That actually sounds like it might work," Pinta nodded.

"We sure better hope it does," Goose nodded.

Goose got up and headed for the restroom where he could place a discreet call to Luther without being disturbed. It wasn't a call he really wanted to make, but it might be a call that would keep him from getting killed.

~ ~ ~

Mary Norman easily mixed in with the other young

women in the bar, though she was easily a decade older than most, she didn't look it. She worked out religiously and ate right to keep herself fit, plus she loved to dance. Even when it wasn't around a pole, men noticed her when she did.

She had started a conversation with a young woman in her mid-twenties named Jesse Carlton. Jessie was blond and vivacious, with grey-blue eyes and a Cupid's bow mouth. High cheekbones and a slightly up-turned nose completed the picture.

"I heard there was quite a party in here last night," Mary said.

"I'll say! John Irwin, Arnie Grossman, Herb Gore, Fabian Morales, the rich boys landed," Jesse said as she took a drink from her fresh cosmopolitan.

"Did they have fun?"

"I'll say they did! They were hitting on all of the girls, and Grossman was the biggest flirt of the bunch. He was all over Tiffany Mendez most of the night, then he said something and she walked off. Right after that a couple of his buddies helped him out to a cab and sent him home," Jesse explained.

"Is Tiffany here tonight?" Mary asked looking around.

"No. She got a phone call about half an hour later and left in a hurry. I've not seen her in here tonight, so far," Jesse admitted. She took another sip of her drink.

"Sounds like I came in on the wrong night," Mary took a drink of her own.

"I think you'll do okay, Mary. That hunk over there can barely take his eyes off of you," Jesse nodded her head toward where Chandler stood across the room.

"He's nice enough I guess," Mary replied, hiding a grin.

"If you don't go after him, I might take a run myself. He looks like a man who could make a woman scream all night long!"

"I'll let you know," Mary replied, starting across the room. As a dancer, Mary knew exactly what it would take to get the focus of everyman in the room on her hips and she worked it, heading towards Chandler like a guided missile. She looked up at him. "Time to go, you're exciting the natives a little too much."

"Like you're not?" he smiled and slipped his arms around her and gave her a long drawn out kiss. When the kiss broke, they headed for the door. The bar had gone silent during that kiss except for the guy singing on the karaoke machine.

Chandler helped her into the Bronco and then walked around to the driver's side. He got the impression that they were being watched. The difficult part about spotting surveillance, especially in the dark, is that the shadows work better to conceal the person or person's doing the watching. He opened his door and climbed in.

"I think we've got company," he said as he started the Ford SUV.

"There's never a dull moment around you," Mary shook her head, an amused expression on her face.

"So far, all they are doing is watching. Unless they make a move on us before we get home, they can continue to watch and we'll see what happens tomorrow."

"That sounds like a good plan."

~ ~ ~

"Luther, some guy on the phone says he's got something you need to hear," Chopper Quinn called.

"Bring me da phone den," Luther said, his voice soft and quiet.

"Sure thing, Boss," Quinn said as he carried the cordless device over to the big black man sitting in the heavy oak chair. The baseball game was still on and the Cubs were getting their asses handed to them by the Detroit Tigers.

"Speak," Luther said into the handset.

"Mister Donlley, my name is Goose. There was some guy down here earlier at the Red Garter asking a bunch of questions about you," Goose stammered.

"What did this man look like?" Luther asked, his voice still soft-spoken.

"He was a big black man, brown hair cut close, white teeth, dressed in real fine looking clothes," Goose said.

"He leave a name?"

"No Sir, he didn't. But he seemed awfully interested in finding out about you."

"I'll remember this Goose," Luther promised him.

"Thank you, Mr. Donlley," Goose said as he hung up. Luther looked at Chopper.

"You know some street punk goes by the name of Goose?" Luther asked.

"I know who he is."

"Find him and kill him. He's been running his mouth. Also, keep an eye out for a big black buck that's been askin' questions about me. I like my privacy," Luther said, his voice still soft, but with an edge of steel to it.

"Right on it, Boss," Chopper nodded, and then he turned and left. Luther frowned. Somebody looking for him, and he didn't know why. He didn't like that one bit. It meant trouble was a comin' one way or another. But was it trouble for him or for Mister Morales? That was something that he would have to ruminate about for a spell. Luther popped the top of another Pabst Blue Ribbon and took a drink and returned his attention to the baseball game on the television.

~ ~ ~

The drive home had proven uneventful. Chandler was glad of that. While he was well aware that Mary could handle herself if things got dangerous, he still felt the need to protect her. So, he was glad that nothing happened.

"So, what did we learn tonight?" Mary asked as they entered their home. Simba bounded out to great them, rubbing against their legs and purring loudly.

"Arnie was definitely targeted by Tiffany. According to several guys in the bar, she had rebuffed them and set her sights as soon as he entered," Chandler told her.

"Tiffany's last name was Mendez. And yes, she had set her sights on Arnie. A few of the girls confirmed it," Mary replied.

"That's something. Now we need to look more into Tiffany's background, find out why she was aimed at Arnie," Chandler nodded. He walked into the kitchen and opened the freezer, removing a bottle of Vodka and then two 6-ounce tumblers from the cupboard. Chandler added ice to both and then poured the vodka over them. He handed one to Mary and then took a sip for himself before putting the bottle back into the freezer.

"Seems like a lot to do for a Sunday," Mary sipped her drink.

"It does. But I want to know who framed Arnie and why. That is why we were hired in the first place," Chandler reminded her.

"Yes, it is. But I think that there may be more to this, and I'm pretty sure that you do too."

"You would be right in that surmise."

"So, what would you suggest we do about it?"

"I suggest that we finish our drinks, make love and then sleep on what we have learned. Perhaps in the morning we will have an epiphany of some sort, one that will point us towards a conclusion of some sort," Chandler told her.

"How can I deny such brilliance?" Mary smiled. It was almost like a sunrise.

"You can't," Chandler told her.

~ ~ ~

Goose and Pinta walked out of the Red Garter at closing time. Melody would meet Goose at his apartment later. The downtown was turning into a ghost town at 3 o'clock in the morning. The pair of friends made their way to where they had left Goose's car earlier in the evening.

They were busy laughing and telling jokes and didn't notice the dark shape huddled at the back end of the car. They didn't notice it until the man stood and opened fire with a MAC-10 sub machinegun. They started into a death dance under the multiple impacts of copper-jacketed slugs. Then the shape was gone, melting into shadowed alleys, leaving two dead bodies leaking blood all over the sidewalk.

~ ~ ~

Morning.

Ogden Spears frowned as he looked at the Sunday Edition of the Indianapolis Star. The dead girl that was found at Arnie Grossman's house had made the front page. Given the salacious nature of the case, he wasn't really surprised. He perused the story, noting that it spelled out the facts and pointed no fingers, other than to offer speculation as to how the dead woman may have gotten there. Spears tossed the paper down in disgust. This wasn't good news, not at all. Arnie Grossman was the face for the new civic centers. Until now, his reputation had been spotless. But with this, they might have to remove Arnie from the project. He took a gulp of his coffee and reached for his telephone. He needed to talk to the others, see how they wanted to handle this!

~ ~ ~

Fabian Morales opened his eyes to the morning sun. Sunday Morning was a new day. He stretched and yawned as he sat up in his bed. He would make some calls. If the police had not arrested Arnie Grossman yet, they would soon.

He had set things up so that he could take over the Civic Centers and put the youth of Indianapolis to work for him, pushing his drugs to the masses. It was a simple plan, one that he was sure that would work.

Arnie Grossman would take the fall, and he, Morales would take over the city. He would rebuild the Circle in his own image.

~ ~ ~

Mary had breakfast cooking on the stove when Chandler emerged from the bedroom. She was just finishing pouring him a cup of coffee and setting it on the table in front of him. She watched, amused, as he added four packs of sweeteners, and stirred them in. He took his first sip and sighed.

"Take a look at the front page of the Star. I think we might be facing a bigger problem," Mary told him.

"The story broke?" Chandler looked at her. Her back was towards him as she was flipping eggs.

"Yes, you could say that," Mary replied over her shoulder.

"How bad is it?"

"Not as bad as it could be. So far, it's mainly facts. But there were a few speculations in the article. I suspect we may want to see how we need to proceed after you read it for yourself."

"That sounds like a good idea."

"The paper is on the coffee table. Go read while I get our plates ready," Mary told him. Chandler nodded his agreement as he headed out of the kitchen. Simba looked up at him, as Chandler took a seat on the couch.

"Mrrow?" Simba regarded him.

"Probably," Chandler told the cat.

Chapter Ten

"John, have you seen this morning's paper yet?" Ogden Spears' voice asked through the phone. John Irwin rolled to a sitting position on the side of the bed.

"Not yet, Ogden. You just woke me up," Irwin growled irritably.

"Then go, take a look, and call me right back. This is going to be a problem for us," Spears said, hanging up. Grumbling, Irwin put his bare feet into his slippers and stood. Despite Ogden's urgent entreaties, John Irwin was not going to rush to the front door and grab the newspaper. He headed for the bathroom first. His wife continued to snore away the morning in their warm bed. Irwin liked sleeping in on Sunday morning, and Ogden was not going to be happy once Irwin voiced his displeasure at the early morning awakening.

If it were football season rather than the start of baseball season, Irwin would have been up for three or four hours already. The Irwin's had owned the Stallions for nearly fifty years, and they had managed a few championships over that time. This year, they were in the hunt again, or would be. But pre-season was still three months away. Irwin took care of business in the bathroom before heading downstairs to get the Indianapolis Star.

~ ~ ~

"Where do we start this morning?" Mary asked.

"I've been thinking about that," Chandler replied as

he took another drink of coffee. "And what have you decided?"

"We need to know more about the dead girl. I want you to see what you can find out about her. I'm going to go see our client and get his response to the newspaper, see if he has managed to remember anything else. I'll probably swing by and see if Detective Cruz has anything new."

"Do you expect him to be in on a Sunday?"

"A high-profile case like this? Yes, I do."

"Okay, I'll see what I can find and let you know. What else do you want to do today?"

"Maybe a picnic on the canal later?"

"I'll see what I can whip up," Mary smiled.

~ ~ ~

The sun was shining and the temperature was rising as Chandler headed his SUV towards the downtown. Sunday morning traffic was still light since it wasn't time for the churchgoers to hit the road yet. Sampson had put Arnie up at the J. W. Marriott. Chandler used the parking garage. Chandler picked up a complimentary newspaper on the way up to Grossman's room. He pounded on it heavily until he heard someone stumbling around and cursing from inside. Finally, the door swung open and a sleepy-eyed Arnie Grossman stood there.

Grossman's hair was disheveled from sleep, his eyes red and bleary. His bare chest was pale white like the belly of a fish, with a few dark scraggly chest hairs poking out. His gut hung over the waistband of his pajamas. "What the hell?" he demanded.

"I would have figured after Friday night that you

would have sworn off the booze for at least a couple of days," Chandler said as he pushed his way inside.

"Chandler?" Arnie sounded confused. He closed the door and followed Chandler inside.

"Arnie, didn't Sampson tell you to lay off the booze?" Chandler asked.

"He may have mentioned it," Arnie winced.

"Put on some coffee. We have things to talk about."

"Sure thing," Arnie headed back towards the suite's kitchen.

"Tell me about Friday, Arnie," Chandler said. He took a seat at the kitchen table as Arnie Grossman went through the motions to get coffee on to brew.

"I told you, I don't remember Friday night."

"What about before Friday night? What about Friday during the day?"

"Why?"

"Because I want to know. Something had to precipitate the events of Friday night. If I knew what that was, I might be well able to figure why that poor young woman was savagely murdered in your living room," Chandler told him. Precipitate. Mary would be proud of him for using big words.

"I guess that sounds reasonable," Arnie nodded as he pressed the button to start the coffee brewing. He got a glass from the cupboard and opened the fridge. He pulled out a bottle of orange juice and filled the glass. He shut the door and walked to the table, sipping at the juice. He took a seat across from Chandler.

"Had you ever met Tiffany Mendez before you went to Land Sharks?" Chandler asked. Arnie took another sip of juice, making a face at how tart it tasted.

"I think I might have," Arnie said finally. The sound of dripping coffee was audible and the aroma of fresh brewed coffee was filling the room.

"Do you remember where you might have met her?" Chandler asked him.

"I'm thinking," Arnie said softly. His brow knitted in concentration as he tried to remember. Chandler waited quietly, not offering to prompt him.

"I think it was about a month ago, at one of the early fund-raisers for the Civic Centers," Arnie said.

"Okay, that is something," Chandler nodded. Arnie sipped some more orange juice. The coffee stopped dripping.

"You want a cup?" Arnie asked him, awake and moving into the role of benevolent host.

"Please," Chandler nodded. Arnie stood and got out a mug, filling it most of the way up and then carrying it back to the table and setting it in front of Chandler. He got a spoon out and slid it across the table. Chandler emptied four packets of artificial sweetener into the coffee and stirred it in. That done he took a tentative sip. Not bad. "So, you had prior contact with her?"

"I guess. I don't remember getting her name, though."

"But you saw her, and recognized her?"

"I guess so," Arnie shrugged.

"So, when she approached you Friday night, you had a sense of who she was?"

"I guess so," Arnie shrugged.

"You weren't surprised to see her there?" Chandler asked.

"Not really, no. I meet a lot of people every day,

Chandler. Some make an impression, some don't," Arnie said.

"I get that, Arnie. Except, this young woman died in your house. She bled out on your living room carpet. Somebody is responsible for that. Don't you even want to know why?" Chandler asked.

"You know I do," Arnie looked contrite.

"Then maybe you should start acting like it, Arnie. I want to know everything you can tell me about Tiffany Mendez."

~ ~ ~

Steve Dickerson looked up as Alejandro Cruz entered the squad room. It was a Sunday and the room was mostly empty. "You got anything?" Dickerson asked.

"I got a lot, but none of it ties together," Cruz told him as he dropped into his chair.

"Do you think this Grossman guy killed her?"

"No, not after talking to him. The poor bastard was set up."

"You seem sure of that."

"I am."

"So, what do you think is going on?" Dickerson asked.

"I wish that I knew. You catch the call on that double homicide last night near the Red Garter?"

"I did. A couple of street punks, gunned down for no apparent reason," Dickerson shrugged.

"You sure about that?" Cruz asked.

"I am."

"I want you to work your sources and make sure," Cruz told him.

"I can do that."

~ ~ ~

Mary Norman frowned at the computer screen. She was actually surprised at how little information that there was about Tiffany Mendez in cyberspace. Her web presence had only been established five years before. That seemed odd for a twenty-something who was trying to make her place in the world.

Investigations in the computer age had become very simple since there was very little that was not on-line about anyone. Anybody that had no cyber-footprint was certainly suspect in the information age. It prompted her to check into other databases that were on the Dark Web. Perhaps she would find something there.

~ ~ ~

"I don't like it," John Irwin said.

"I'm not asking you to like it John. But I am asking you to consider what we might be facing," Ogden Spears told him.

"I know very well what we might be facing, Ogden. I just don't care! I like Arnie, and I'm willing to back him, regardless of how this mess plays out," Irwin said.

"I wish the other investors felt the same," Spears groused.

"Those other investors need to grow a pair," Irwin growled.

"Perhaps. I'll stand with you for now," Spears said.

"I thought you might," Irwin said.

~ ~ ~

As the Owner and General Manager of the Indianapolis Stallions, John Irwin was a major power player in Central Indiana. He and Spears had been friends for a long time. More years than either of them cared to remember.

John Irwin wished that it were in the season. Alas it wasn't. It was spring training, and he could still easily change the team line-up and the players were just chess pieces on a board.

John had worked hard to get funding for the Civic Centers. They were something near and dear to him. He had once been a player that nobody had thought was worth anything, not until he had managed to pull on pads and get into a game. He had never made the pros, but he had been recognized at the college level.

That had been enough to please the Old Man. But in the end, it had not been enough. Not for him to be able to please himself. So, when he had taken over the ownership of the team, he had worked hard to make them champions. They would be champions again. John Irwin wanted to help the city. He wasn't about to let Arnie Grossman's misfortune get in the way of that!

Chapter Eleven

Rather than a picnic on the canal, Mary had opted for them to go to Victory Field and watch a baseball game between the Indianapolis Indians and the Toledo Mud Hens. They had watched and cheered as Barnett Barnes hit a sacrifice fly to drive in Austin Meadows at the bottom of the 11th to cap off a 3-2 walk-off win, which put the Indians on an 8-game consecutive win streak for the first time since the 2014 season.

"That was fun," Mary said as she leaned against him while they made their way out of the ballpark.

"Yes, it was. We need to do this more often," Chandler agreed.

"You like sports. Yet you never insist that we watch them," Mary looked up at him with her deep blue eyes.

"Why would I?"

"Perhaps because you know that I enjoy things that we can do together?"

"I don't like to superimpose the things that I like on our relationship. I know you enjoy going to Museums, eating out, theatre, and the like," Chandler shrugged.

"So, you are suppressing your own likes to conform to my likes?" Mary looked at him.

"Not consciously," Chandler admitted.

"Phil, we work because we complement each other. I like sports and I am more than happy to go or watch sporting events with you," Mary said.

"I know that. I also know that I like doing things you like."

"Except I don't want you to forego what you like to please me. In doing that, you are suppressing your own desires, and if you do that, you will eventually come to resent me," Mary said.

"I will never resent you, Mary," Chandler told her.

"You say that now."

"For me, it is an empirical truth."

"For now."

"Forever."

"Phil, we both know better. We need to be totally honest with each other all the time in order for what we have to work. Do you agree?"

"I suppose so."

"Have you been totally honest with me so far?"

"As much as I could be," Chandler sighed.

"I know that you love me. I also know that you still love and miss the wife and the daughter that you had before you met me. I cannot and will not ever replace them. But I will do what I can to make your life complete going forward," Mary said.

"That does make sense," Chandler nodded. "So where do we go from here?"

"We go home and we wake up together tomorrow and start a new day," Mary said softly.

"That sounds like a really good idea."

~ ~ ~

A car was parked out front when they got back home. It took a moment for Chandler to recognize Johnny Quick's Crossfire. "Company?" Mary asked.

"Johnny," Chandler replied.

"Ah. Did you invite him over?"

"No, but I'm sure he has a reason."

"So, let's find out what it is," Mary opened the door and climbed out of the Bronco. She had met Johnny Quick when they were trying to clear a professional basketball player of murdering his girlfriend. He had saved Chandler's life in a shootout in Methodist Hospital with a bunch of Detroit Mobsters. It had been their only interaction. She was curious about the man.

Chandler opened his door and exited the Bronco as well. Johnny was leaning on the rear fender of his car. "Chandler," he smiled.

"Hey Johnny. You know Mary of course?" Chandler said.

"We've met. You got a good one in her," Johnny nodded.

"I know that. You have something for me?"

"Better we talk inside," Johnny said.

"We can do that. The Indians beat the Mud Hens if you're interested."

"That'll make my bookie happy," Johnny said as they headed up the walk. Mary opened the door and stepped inside, heading for the kitchen. Simba looked up from where he was curled up on the couch. "Mrrow?"

"Behave," Chandler told the orange tabby cat.

"You got a pet?" Johnny seemed surprised.

"You seem surprised."

"I am, you don't seem the type. I'd have figured you for a guard dog or something like that."

"Dogs are over-rated."

"I guess," Johnny shook his head.

"Would you like coffee or a beer?" Mary asked from

the kitchen.

"Coffee is good," Johnny replied.

"So, what have you got?" Chandler asked.

"I got a guy from around 10th and Rural named Luther Donlley. Seems he be the man running the black gangs in town, and from what I hear, he be running them for Fabian Morales," Johnny said.

"That is pretty interesting news," Chandler nodded.

"I told you Morales was dirty," Mary cut in as she came out with two cups of coffee on saucers. She handed one to each of them before disappearing back into the kitchen.

"You think this Luther Donlley killed the girl?" Chandler asked him.

"I think he could be good for it," Johnny said.

"That is certainly something to look into. You pick up any talk about the dead girl?"

"Not yet."

"Keep looking," Chandler said.

"No problem," Johnny flashed him a grin.

"How do you like Indianapolis?" Mary asked as she walked back in with her own cup of coffee.

"It's growing on me," Johnny offered her a smile.

"Can you explain this bond you two share?"

"Nothing to explain. Chandler do what he says he'll do. Same with me. We both know it, so we don't have to talk about it," Johnny told her.

"Even if it confuses the people around you?" Mary asked. "Even then," Johnny smiled.

"You two make an interesting study."

"Glad I can be of service," Johnny smiled at her.

~ ~ ~

Luther Donlley wasn't happy. He had read through the newspaper. The girl's death was going to bring too much heat down on them. He had warned Fabian that might happen, but the goddam spic hadn't cared. He had just gone ahead and done it anyway.

Luther couldn't understand why Morales had felt the need to put Grossman out as a sacrificial animal. It was grandstanding in the worst possible way. It was going to put them under a microscope. Oh well, that just meant he would have to make things happen to divert the cops' attention.

~ ~ ~

"Fabian, I'm just not sure this is the way to go," Ogden Spears shook his head. It was Sunday night and the two were having a late meal at Prime 47 on South Pennsylvania Ave.

"Ogden, it's quite obvious that Arnie lost control and murdered that poor girl. He probably arranged for her to come to his home before you put him in that cab," Morales sighed.

"Maybe, Fabian. But I'm not quite ready to write Arnie off yet. He's done a lot of good for this town. These Civic Centers are just the start," Ogden Spears told him.

"Do the others feel the same?" Morales asked him.

"The ones I have spoken with, do," Spears said.

"If this is not cleared up soon, Ogden, I am afraid I might have to withdraw my support of the project."

"That would be a blow, Fabian, but it would not be insurmountable. I can easily find others willing to invest in the city. I don't want to have to do that, but I can."

"That sounds almost like a threat, Ogden."

"It's no threat, Fabian. Just a fact."

"You have until the end of the week. If this isn't resolved, I will withdraw all of my capital." Morales said, standing. He turned and marched out, leaving Spears to pick up the check.

"Asshole," Spears said, watching him go.

~ ~ ~

"Your friend is an interesting man," Mary said as she sat on the couch. Chandler was watching NCIS: Los Angeles.

"Johnny certainly is that," Chandler acknowledged.

"I think I u nderstand the two of you a little more now."

"Is that a good thing or a bad one?"

"That, I haven't decided on yet."

"Why not?"

"Woman's prerogative."

"That's really not an answer," Chandler told

"It's the only answer that you'll get," Mary said.

"Is that fair?"

"Life's not fair."

"No, it is not, but it is what it is. Is that what you're telling me?"

"That, Lover, is for you to decide."

~ ~ ~

Steve Dickerson frowned as he once more read over the report on the murder downtown. He recognized the names of a couple of low-life gang members. For the life of him, he couldn't figure out who would want to hit the two of them.

They were nickel and dimmers at best. They had never gotten involved in anything that would warrant a hit of this proportion. He looked over at his partner. Alejandro Cruz was at his desk even if it was a Sunday night.

"You were asking me about the shooting outside the Red Garter. Was there a reason for it?" Dickerson asked.

"More a hunch than a reason," Cruz told him.

"Talk to me partner," Dickerson said.

"I think it might tie into the Arnie Grossman case," Cruz explained.

"How do you figure that?" Dickerson asked.

"Because, I think those two had something to do with the death of Tiffany Mendez," Cruz sighed.

"I thought that the rich guy did it?" Dickerson looked confused.

"The evidence doesn't support that," Cruz told him.

"Why are you just telling me this now?"

"Because I just confirmed it."

"Okay, that's a good reason," Dickerson nodded.

Chapter Twelve

Tiffany Mendez had lived in the Wellington Square Apartments on East 64th Street. Mary had given him the address after breakfast and he wanted to check the place out. Mary would get the office open and pursue some other areas of the investigation, but Chandler needed to know more about the dead girl.

It bothered him that Arnie had lied about not knowing her the first time that they had talked. He planned to mention that to Larry Sampson when he stopped by his office later. After all, he had gotten Larry involved with Arnie. Larry deserved to know the truth.

The prior knowledge of the girl bothered Chandler, and it made him doubt everything that his Client had told him. The murder charges began and ended with the dead girl. To find the truth, Chandler had to find out more about her.

He doubted that Cruz had been around yet. He would be waiting until this morning when he could get a judge to sign a warrant to allow him to search the dead girl's apartment. Fortunately, Chandler didn't need a warrant. He planned to be in and out again before Cruz ever got around to searching the place.

Her apartment was on the ground floor at the back of the building. Chandler had parked his Jeep Cherokee outside. He carried a small parcel under his arm as he entered the building, doing his best to look like a deliveryman. He carried the parcel to her door and knocked. No answer. Good, that meant no roommate. He pulled out his lock picks and went to work on the door. He was inside in less than half a minute.

Chandler shut the door behind him and flipped up the light switch. Dim lights recessed in the ceiling flared to life. Chandler tossed the bogus package on a small table near the door. The décor was decidedly feminine, not surprising really.

A small kitchen table sat in the dining area, a couch and chairs were lined up in front of a small flat screen TV. A small writing desk sat in the corner, set up with a PC, monitor, and printer. He would check those in a few minutes. He headed back to the bedroom.

The bedroom held a single bed and a dresser. Chandler looked them over. Nothing interesting on top. He began to go through the drawers of the dresser. Nothing there. He moved to the bathroom.

The medicine chest held no surprises, a razor, shaving cream, vitamins, birth control pills, tampons. Nothing that helped. Other than he knew at least that she was sexually active. Chandler headed back to the living room.

"Shawn, I want you to run by the girl's place, make sure she didn't leave nothing behind that will lead back to us," Luther Donlley said.

"Sure thing. You care if I take 3-bop along?" Shawn asked.

"Keep him from shooting anyone. We don't need the extra heat," Luther replied.

"Sho' thing," Shawn nodded, grabbing his friend and heading out the door.

Luther figured that trouble was coming. It would be

because of killing that girl. Morales couldn't see it, but he wasn't down on the street like Luther was. He thought he was above it all. 'Cepting Luther knew better. It might come time that he'd have to remind Morales of that.

~ ~ ~

Johnny Quick had found him a good parking spot where he could watch the house where Luther Donlley stayed. He had asked around and found that Luther pretty much controlled whatever went on along 10th Street.

There were good people and bad in the 'hood, but Luther ran the bad. The good folk tried to stay the hell out of his way. Most of the time they could, but not always. Luther's Goons patrolled the street, and even the cops seemed to fight shy of them. Johnny didn't like that.

Maybe it was because of his own upbringing on the streets of Detroit. He knew what it was like to be scared of the gangs, to wonder if he would live to make it home from school on any given day, or if he would be gunned down in a drive-by as he walked home from school. Johnny had made it out by playing ball.

He had talent. The heads of the local gang recognized that. They figured if they backed him, they could get a piece of him if he went pro. When he did, they had tried. But Johnny hadn't let them force him to throw games. They had murdered his sister, trying to teach him a lesson. It didn't take.

Johnny quit the team and tracked each of the gang members down and killed them. That had brought him to the attention of the Detroit Mob. Johnny had gone to work for them. Until Chandler.

He shook his head at the memory. Dominic Jones. The kid was a fucking natural. He had it all. The skills, the drive, but he refused to shave points. So, the mob had murdered his girlfriend and put the blame on him. Except the kid had hired Chandler. Chandler had taken out the hitmen sent after the kid and exonerated him in the murder of his girlfriend.

It seemed like eons, but in fact it had only been a few months. Johnny owed Chandler for saving the kid. He shook his head. He climbed out of the car and walked across the street. It was time to beard the lion in his den!

~ ~ ~

Alejandro Cruz walked out of the courthouse. He had a warrant for the dead woman's apartment. He hoped to find something there that would reveal why she had turned up dead in Arnie Grossman's apartment.

This case was political; he had felt that from the beginning. It reminded him of the first case he had worked with Chandler, the one that had exposed The Circle as the secret, hidden government behind the City of Indianapolis.

~ ~ ~

Chandler was just getting ready to leave when he heard a noise from the front door. Somebody was trying to pick the lock. Judging from the trouble they were having, they weren't very good at it. It was still too early for the cops to have gotten here, though he was sure that they wouldn't be much longer. Chandler drew his Colt Commander .45 and crouched down in a corner. The lock clicked and the door swung open.

Two young black guys in their mid-twenties entered. The one in back bobbing his head in time to music from the iPod in his pocket. He appeared to be wearing Earbuds. The one in the front was putting away a lock pick set. "Shut the door, 3-bop. We need to make sure that girl didn't leave nothing behind," he said.

"Who are you guys?" Chandler said, stepping out into the light, the .45 leading the way. 3-bop and Shawn froze.

"Who the fuck are you?" Shawn asked

"I'm the guy asking the questions," Chandler replied. Just then a gun appeared in 3-bop's hand and it spit flame and lead at him.

"Shit!" Chandler snarled as he dropped to the floor, firing as he went down. Shawn screamed and spun around as the guy behind him sprayed lead through the apartment. Chandler rolled for cover as bullets ripped the air above him. Then both of the intruders were gone and it grew quiet except for the ringing in his ears. Chandler performed a tactical magazine change, replacing the partially spent one with a full one. Then he climbed to his feet and walked to the door.

The two men were gone, but a few of the neighbors were timidly peeking out through partially cracked open doors. Chandler looked at them. "Could somebody please call the police?"

~ ~ ~

"Why am I not surprised to find you here in the middle of this?" Alejandro Cruz asked when he arrived.

"Maybe because you know me?" Chandler shrugged.

"I know you've already been through the place. Did you find anything helpful?"

"Not really, no. She had a date book and had scribbled a note about going to Land Sharks because she had heard that Grossman was going to be there. That's about it."

"What about the shooters?"

"Never saw them before. But one of them did say that they needed to make sure that she hadn't left anything around that might come back on their boss," Chandler said. He had pulled out a toothpick and was chewing on it in the corner of his mouth.

"Frankly, I'm surprised there isn't a body here," Cruz gave him the cop deadeye stare. It didn't faze him.

"I winged one of them, but the other guy was spraying so much lead around that I was busy trying to find cover and not catch any of it."

"Think if you looked at mug shots you could pick them out?"

"Probably."

"Head downtown. I'll call Dickerson and have him show you the books."

"I'm not your enemy here, Alejandro. I want to find out who killed that girl as much as you do. However, I don't believe Arnie Grossman did it," Chandler said.

"I think you might be right, but I don't have evidence to back that opinion up. Find the proof and I'll do my best to help you."

"I know that. Mary sends her regards," Chandler told him.

"She's a good woman, Chandler."

"She is. That's why I love her."

"This case has me worried."

"Why is that?"

"Because there are a lot of political pressures on this. These people, the ones involved, they make me think of the Circle," Cruz sighed.

"It does have that feel. Do you think somebody is trying to rebuild the Circle?" Chandler asked softly.

"Yeah, I do."

"I'll keep my ears open. Call Dickerson, tell him I should be there in about 45 minutes," Chandler said, heading for the door.

"Okay," Cruz replied, pulling out his cell.

~ ~ ~

Johnny Quick was back at 10th and Rural, keeping an eye on the house that housed Luther Donlley. He had a feeling about that old man. It wasn't a good one. Johnny knew from his own upbringing in Detroit that each gang had a leader. He had a feeling that Luther Donlley was one such leader. Even the leaders had bosses. Fabian Morales had the feel of being one of those leaders.

Quick had listened to what Mary Norman had to say about her interview with the Mexican Entrepreneur. He knew that what Mary had picked up on was because of her own street smarts. Chandler might not understand it, but Johnny did. He had grown up on the streets as well.

~ ~ ~

Arnie Grossman sat on the bed in his hotel room. He had taken what Chandler had told him to heart. He hadn't gotten drunk the night before. He was in trouble. He knew that. More trouble than he had ever been in before.

Yes, he had known Tiffany. She was a good person.

He had liked her because she made him feel normal. She had liked him for who he was and not for his money. Now she was dead. It was his fault. Arnie was sure of that. If she hadn't been interested in him, she would probably still be alive.

How could he have been so stupid? It seemed a reasonable question. Arnie shook his head. All he wanted to do was help people. Now he was a murder suspect, and his friends were all running for cover, afraid of being tarred by the same brush.

~ ~ ~

Mary had decided to do some digging into the background of Fabian Morales. Chandler would probably be pissed when he found out. But she couldn't help herself. Morales had frightened her. He had frightened her in a way that she never wanted to be frightened again.

On the surface, Morales seemed clean. But once she dug a little deeper, a far different picture emerged. Morales was quite a bit more than a benevolent figure. He was a drug dealer, and he ran gangs that participated in murder for hire and strong-arm activities. To Mary's way of thinking, Morales was a devil. He ripped people's souls out to force them to do his bidding. She shivered as she read the reports. She hit print, so that she could present them to Chandler when he got back to the office.

~ ~ ~

Steve Dickerson looked up as Phillip Chandler walked into the Homicide Bullpen. Cruz had called ahead and told him to expect Chandler. But this was the first time that he had laid eyes on the guy. Seeing him, he began to understand Chandler's reputation.

Chapter Thirteen

"Chandler?" Steve Dickerson asked, standing and extending his hand. Chandler shook it and took the seat across the desk from him.

"I'm sure Alejandro has told you that I am a major pain in his ass," Chandler chuckled as he sat.

"More than once. But he also said you are damn good at what you do and he'd trust you with his life," Dickerson replied.

"That he's right about. He wants me to look at mug books and see if I can identify the two guys that started shooting at me in Tiffany Mendez's apartment."

"That would certainly be helpful, though I gotta tell you he likes your friend Arnie for it."

"He's wrong."

"He said you'd say that."

"Don't worry, I'll prove it."

"Maybe," Dickerson shrugged.

"No maybe to it," Chandler told him.

~ ~ ~

Luther Donlley picked up the telephone. "Luther, we got trouble," Shawn groaned.

"What happened," Luther asked softly.

"Some guy was in the apartment when we got there. He started shooting, got me in the shoulder and 3-bop shot back. I need a fucking doctor."

"Go see Monroe. He'll take care of you. Send 3-

bop to me. I want him to describe the shooter. Somebody is messing with us and I don't like it," Luther commanded.

"Okay, Shawn replied before hanging up.

Luther frowned. Shit was starting to get out of hand, all because of that damn girl Morales wanted killed and dumped in the rich guy's house. Morales was gonna get them all killed or thrown in jail. Maybe it was time to do something about him!

~ ~ ~

Larry Sampson frowned as he read the e-mail that Mary Norman had just sent him, detailing the fact that Arnie Grossman had indeed met Tiffany Mendez before that Friday night celebration at Land Sharks. If Chandler had uncovered that fact, it was likely that the cops would too. It would make the defense harder, but not impossible. He e-mailed Mary back asking for more details. The more he knew about it before confronting his client, the better it would be. As it was, he still didn't believe that Arnie had killed the girl, but this information had lessened his faith in his client's honesty.

~ ~ ~

"Yeah, I know both of those guys. They work for a guy named Luther Donlley he runs most of the black gangs in town. Bloods, Crips, Eastside, Westside, it doesn't matter. They all answer to Luther," Dickerson said as he looked at the two men that Chandler had identified.

"Tell me about this Luther Donlley," Chandler said.

"Luther runs all the black gangs in town. He's like a counselor to them all, makes peace when there is a problem, but all of them will line up for war if he calls them. He's been around forever and they all respect him," Dickerson explained.

"If his boys are interested in Tiffany Mendez, he sounds like somebody I should talk to," Chandler observed.

"I wouldn't advise it. Even the boys in our department wouldn't go after him without a full SWAT roll out."

"A real bad ass then?"

"And then some."

"Good to know," Chandler said as he stood.

"You're going to go see him," Dickerson said. There was no question to it.

"Seems like I should," Chandler shrugged.

"Good luck," Dickerson told him.

"Luck ain't got nothing to do with it," Chandler told him, before turning and heading out. Dickerson watched him go, shaking his head. He could tell Chandler was a hardass, but he wondered if he was really hard enough to go after Luther Donlley.

~ ~ ~

Chandler walked out of the Metro station and pulled out his cell phone. Johnny was looking at Donlley, and he wanted to give him an update. Donlley was definitely somebody that they wanted to talk to, though he was pretty sure that Donlley wouldn't want to talk to them.

"Go," Quick said when he answered.

"You got eyes on that house?" Chandler asked.

"I do."

"Keep on it then. I'll be along shortly. We need to

talk to this guy."

"It won't be easy."

"If it was easy, I'd handle it myself," Chandler told him.

"Right."

"I shot it out with a couple of his boys this morning. I don't like him, but we need to have a talk with him."

"Sounds reasonable," Johnny replied.

"Good. Make sure that he doesn't leave before I get there."

"I can do that," Johnny told him.

~ ~ ~

Alejandro Cruz finished up at the dead girl's apartment. He carried her laptop with him when he left. He didn't believe that Chandler had found nothing of interest other than a notation in her personal calendar. No, he was sure that the laptop held secrets that would be telling. He had pocketed the personal calendar as well.

The sun was still bright in the sky and the heat of the day was building when he stepped outside and headed towards his unmarked car. He heard the sound of a car speeding up in the parking lot and looked up. That's when he saw the gun sticking out of the window of the car racing towards him.

Cruz dropped to one knee and drew his pistol, stabbing it towards the car and stroking the trigger. He fired again as the gunner in the car fired. The laptop went flying away, struck by the shooter's bullet. Glass shattered and the car sped off. Cruz looked at the shattered laptop and began to curse. He walked to his car to radio it in.

~ ~ ~

The sky was starting to cloud over when Chandler pulled his Jeep Cherokee in behind Johnny's Crossfire. Johnny got out and walked back to where Chandler sat. Chandler stepped out of the Jeep. "He's still in there," Johnny said.

"Good to know. So how about we go talk to him?"

"Sounds like a fine idea to me," Johnny smiled, flashing even white teeth. Together they crossed 10th street and walked up the sidewalk to the house. Chandler drew his .45 and stepped to the side. Johnny rang the bell and knocked on the door, then stepped out of the view of the peephole in the door. Johnny pulled out a Ruger GP-100 with a 6-inch barrel, chambered in .357 Magnum.

They waited. Finally, the door started to open. Chandler stepped around and helped it along with a hard kick! The door flew open and the two men pushed inside. A teenage black man lay on the floor groaning from where the door had impacted against his face. Johnny kicked him in the head as they passed, rendering him unconscious.

The duo moved deeper into the house. "Theo, who was at the door?" called a soft voice.

"Avon calling," Chandler said as he let his .45 lead the way into the room. Johnny filled the doorway behind him, his Ruger leading the way.

"Who the hell are you?" Luther Donlley asked as he stood to face them. He held no weapon.

"We are a couple of guys that need to speak to you," Chandler told him.

"You the one that's been asking after me," Luther

said, eyeing Johnny.

"I am."

"I don't know you, white bread," Luther said, looking at Chandler.

"No, you don't. But I know you, Luther," Chandler replied soberly.

"Do tell," Luther said.

"You know a girl named Tiffany Mendez?" Chandler asked.

"I know a lot of girls."

"Do you know Tiffany?"

"Why would it matter?"

"She's dead. I think you have something to do with it," Chandler told him.

"I got nothing to do with any dead people. I'm just an old man trying to get by."

"I don't believe you for a minute."

"I guess that's up to you," Luther shrugged.

"I guess it is," Chandler said.

"I don't like people asking about me. I like my privacy," Luther said. He was looking at Johnny when he said it.

"Too bad. I don't give up when I take an interest in folks," Johnny said. Something passed between the two, and Chandler wasn't sure what it was, but he knew it wasn't good!

"Hope you got your life insurance paid up, boy."

"I could say the same for you," Johnny smiled, flashing his teeth.

"Get the hell out of my house," Luther told them.

"We will, for now," Chandler told him. He and Johnny backed down the hallway and out the front door. They walked to their vehicles and drove away. Luther watched them go with an angry gaze. He didn't like being disrespected in his own home.

~ ~ ~

"So, what you think?" Johnny asked after they pulled into a McDonalds and went inside to order. Johnny got a big Mac with everything while Chandler opted for a double bacon Cheeseburger and fries. They both got Sprite to drink.

"I think he knows a hell of a lot more than he told us," Chandler said, while biting into his sandwich.

"He does. He made it personal between me and him in there," Johnny said. He took a big bite out of his sandwich and chewed on it.

"I noticed that," Chandler said.

"Man wants a pissing contest, he got it," Johnny said.

"I don't think I like the sound of that."

"You don't have to like it, but it is going to happen."

"I get that."

"You know I got this to do."

"Yeah, I know it. I don't like it, but I know it."

"Then it is best you get out of the way while it happening."

"I figured that out already, Johnny."

"I know that too, Chandler. You do what you gotta, and I be doing the same," Johnny told him.

~ ~ ~

Steve Dickerson got out of the car and approached his partner. Cruz looked as he came towards him. "Al, you get anything?"

"Not enough to matter."

"But you got something?" Dickerson asked.

"Maybe. I had her computer until somebody blasted it out of my hands. I do still have her date book," Cruz told him.

"The forensics people might be able to still get something off what's left of the laptop."

"I hope so," Cruz sighed. This damn case was getting more complicated by the minute.

~ ~ ~

"It's done," Emmett Green's voice sounded in Luther Donlley's ear. "The computer is destroyed. I put a bullet into it."

"I hope so. That girl smart, smarter than she needed to be," Luther said. His hooded eyes were half closed as he pondered his next step. "I want you to find two men for me. One white, one black. They came into the house earlier. Keenan will send you pictures of them. Find them!"

"Sure thing, Boss," Emmett replied, hanging up. Luther put the telephone down and went back to his chair. A young girl came in. She wore a white tee shirt and jeans, flip-flops on her feet. Her curly hair was tied back from her face. It was an innocent face, heart shaped with high cheekbones and café au lait skin. Large brown eyes looked at him. "Can I get you anything, Grampa?" she asked.

"Naw, Darcy, I'm good. Why don't you go and tell Annette to come out here? I got some work for her," Luther told his granddaughter. Darcy nodded and disappeared down the hallway. Moments later another woman appeared. There was a strong resemblance between her and Darcy.

Chapter Fourteen

It was raining by the time Chandler got back to his office. He removed the ball cap that he kept in the Jeep and tossed it onto the coat tree in the corner to dry out. Mary sat at her desk, regarding her computer monitor and looking pensive. "A penny for your thoughts?" he said.

"They really aren't worth that much," she sighed leaning back in her chair.

"Don't sell yourself short, Kid. You're smarter than I am," Chandler told her.

"Liar."

"No, it's true. I've got street smarts, but you've got the book smarts."

"Reverse that statement, Phil. I've never sat foot in an institution of higher learning unless it was to dance at a bachelor party. You had to have a degree to get into the Marshal's service."

"Yes, I did. I also worked in the Military Police as a Marine, which gave me a certain amount of law enforcement experience. I put that to use as a Marshal and I use what I learned on both jobs now in this one," Chandler replied.

"Yes, you do. I use my knowledge of people and human nature to help you," Mary added.

"You do," Chandler agreed. "It is one of many things that I love about you."

"So, what did you find out?" Mary looked at him

expectantly.

"Tiffany did indeed know Arnie prior to that night at Land Sharks which led to her death. Also, she had been informed ahead of time that he would be there that night and was encouraged to approach him and try to get him into a compromising position," Chandler said.

"Encouraged by who?"

"She didn't mention in the computer diary that she kept, but I figure you might be able to delve deeper into that," Chandler removed a thumb drive from his pocket and handed it to her.

"What's this?" Mary looked at him.

"Her digital journal. I copied it before the two shooters showed up."

"Two shooters?" Mary raised an eyebrow.

"Yes, two guys came while I was at Tiffany's apartment. When I confronted them, they started shooting. I winged one of them and then they fled. I called 911 and then had to deal with Alejandro," Chandler told her.

"I'm sure he wasn't happy," Mary rolled her eyes.

"You'd be right, but I did throw him a bone to keep him happy," Chandler grinned.

"Good for you," Mary smiled.

"It was a rare moment for me."

"I'm sure it was."

"Crack that journal. Johnny and I were stirring the pot earlier."

"Stirring the pot how?"

"We braced the head of all the black gangs in the city in his home this morning," Chandler said.

"You did what?" Mary's voice rose in concern.

"We need for somebody to make a move. When they do, it will give us an in to finding out what really happened," Chandler said.

"Phil, I am not sure that was the best idea."

"Maybe not, but it's done. So now we wait and see what happens."

"Crap!" Mary snarled.

~ ~ ~

Johnny Quick watched from down the block as more and more young people entered the house where Luther Donlley lived. The activity made him curious. It was obvious that the gang leader was up to something, the big question was what?

It was a fact that Donlley would send people out looking for him and Chandler. The man was highly offended that the two of them had disrespected him by going after him in his own home. He watched as more people spilled out of the house and began moving along the streets. It was time to go. If he stayed, more than one of them would spot him watching,

~ ~ ~

Fabian Morales was angry. Luther was over-reaching his bounds. By trying to tell him that he had made a mistake killing the girl. Morales was the power behind the throne. He ran the gangs through Luther Donlley. Donlley need to be reminded of that. Morales motioned to Sanchez. Sanchez was a loyal member of his family.

"I want you to kill one of Luther Donlley's family. Do it openly and brutally. It is to serve as a message that he works for me," Morales told him.

"As you wish," Sanchez replied before standing and

exiting the room. Rebuilding the Circle was work, but Morales was well on his way to making it happen. Gore was in. So were the women. John Irwin and Ogden Spears were the only hold outs. But he would draw them in soon enough.

~ ~ ~

Steve Dickerson smiled as he read the e-mail on his monitor. "Alejandro, I have something," he said.

"What?" Cruz asked.

"Tiffany Mendez kept a journal on her laptop. Our forensic people were able to recover it," Dickerson told him.

"That is good news. What does it say?"

"They are still working on that, but they should have something for us by tomorrow."

"I guess that is better than nothing," Cruz sighed.

"It is. You might well be surprised by what we find."

"I might, but there are no guarantees," Cruz told him.

~ ~ ~

Chandler sat back in his chair, his fingers forming a pyramid as he contemplated all that he had learned so far. It was a confusing puzzle and one that did not offer a clear ending. Yet somewhere, out there, were the pieces that would make it fit and offer that final clue to name the killer.

Chandler pulled open the bottom drawer of his desk and pulled out a bottle of Jim Beam and a glass. He poured two fingers into the small tumbler, recapped the bottle and put it back in the drawer. He took a sip, enjoying the burn as it slid down his throat and hit his stomach. He turned on the radio. It was set on 88.5 The

Diamond, a local PBS station that played classical music from midnight to noon, and then jazz from noon until midnight. The jazz portion of the day had just started and John Coltrane's favorite things came out of the speaker. Chandler toasted the radio and took another drink.

So far, he had two suspects for Tiffany's murder other than Arnie Grossman. On one hand, he had Fabian Morales, a great guy until you looked beneath the surface as Mary had done. She had compiled a file that had been waiting on his desk when he got to it. It had provided some very interesting reading.

And then there was Luther Donlley, who seemed to run all of the street level black gangs in Indianapolis. While Donlley ran things, it seemed that the city cops were not aware of him. Chandler wondered about that. He took a drink and picked up the telephone and dialed Alejandro Cruz at the Police department headquarters.

~ ~ ~

Traffic was light in the downtown area at noon, probably due to the rain. Johnny cruised around the circle before heading for Chandler's office. They needed a plan, and he figured between Chandler and Mary, one could be worked out. Donlley was going to be coming for them both. Chandler and Mary both needed to know that.

Plus, he could let Chandler know that Donlley had put the word out. Johnny shook his head. Chandler had really gotten them in deep this time. They could take Luther, but he wasn't sure they could take on an army of gangs.

~ ~ ~

"Cruz," Alejandro answered.

"Hey, Alejandro. I've got something for you," Chandler said.

"What, Chandler, a social disease?" Cruz rolled his eyes.

"You ever hear of a guy named Luther Donlley?" Chandler asked.

"I can't say I have," Cruz replied.

"You might want to take a look at him. He seems to be running all of the black street gangs in the city."

"And you know this how?"

"Because, Quick and I braced him in his house. He lives on 10th Street near Rural."

"If what you're suggesting is true, how come nobody in the department has ever heard of the guy?"

"Maybe they have, and didn't bother to tell anyone."

"Chandler, do you know how you sound right now?"

"Yes. Maybe he was protected by The Circle. And he kept out of sight after we brought them down. But Luther Donlley kept things going, business as usual. I think maybe now he has a new sponsor, somebody trying to rebuild the Circle," Chandler explained.

"Do you know who it is?" Cruz asked, suddenly alert.

"Not yet, but I'm working on it. I think whoever it is was the person responsible for Tiffany Mendez's murder."

"I'll check this Donlley guy out," Cruz said.

"Thank you," Chandler replied and hung up. Cruz sat back in his chair. Chandler had given him a lot to think about. He looked over at Dickerson. "Find me everything we have on a guy named Luther Donlley,"

Cruz said.

~ ~ ~

"Johnny, to what do we owe the pleasure?" Mary Norman smiled as he walked in the door.

"I wish I could say that it was good news," Johnny told her truthfully.

"I wish you could too. However, since we took this case, good news hasn't exactly been a premium. He's back in his office. Have him let me know when you guys want me to come back," Mary told him.

"Why not now?" Johnny looked at her.

"Because I get the feeling he may not take what you have to say well," Mary shrugged.

"You might be right about that," Johnny nodded, heading for the door. He opened it without knocking and stepped inside, shutting the door behind him. Mary looked at the door, took a deep breath and let it out in a long sigh.

~ ~ ~

"Little early for the booze, ain't it?" Johnny asked.

"It's past noon. When did you become my Daddy?" Chandler asked, downing the last of the whiskey. He opened the bottom drawer on his desk and set the glass down inside it, before closing it.

"I ain't your Daddy and never have been. You want to get drunk before quitting that time, that's on you," Quick replied.

"Yes, it is. You got a reason for being here?"

"I do," Quick said.

"So, what is it? Other than to complain about my drinking habits?" Chandler asked.

"Donlley has put the word out on us. His gangs are

all looking," Johnny said.

"We were pretty sure that would happen."

"Yeah, but they ain't going to recognize that Mary is a non-combatant. They gonna figure she's a part of it anyway."

"That would be a big mistake on their part."

"I know that, but they don't."

"What are you suggesting then?"

"Might be a good time for her to take a vacation."

"She'd never agree to that. She's in for a penny, in for a pound," Chandler told him.

"I figured that, but I had to try," Johnny shook his head.

"I know you did, Pal. But it is, what it is."

"I kind of figured that. Chandler, you have to talk to her and get her out of here and get her somewhere safe."

"I would if I could, Johnny."

"I guess I know that."

"I guess you do. This is going to get ugly fast, Chandler," Johnny said.

"I know. I'll tell Mary and let her make her own decision," Chandler told him.

Chapter Fifteen

Mary looked at the two men seated in the office and leaned against the doorframe. "I guess you're ready for me?" Mary looked at them.

"Yes, that's why I asked you to come in," Chandler pointed out the obvious.

"Is there a reason why I have a feeling I'm not going to like what you're about to tell or ask me?"

"There is."

"So, give me the bad news first and hopefully the good news will make up for it."

"Johnny?" Chandler looked over at him.

"Since I'm the one brought the bed news, I guess?" Quick sighed.

"You guessed correctly," Chandler grinned.

"Luther Donlley has put people on the street, looking for me and Chandler. More likely than not, they ain't gonna recognize you as a non-combatant. Your life gonna be in just as much danger as ours, maybe even more," Johnny told her.

"I see," Mary nodded, looking at Chandler. "I suppose you both want to whisk me off somewhere safe to protect me."

"That was the general idea," Chandler admitted.

"Well, you can both forget it! I'm a part of this, whether you like it or not! Does this scare me? You damn well know it does! But that doesn't mean I am going to let you push me out of the case."

"He said you'd say that," Johnny sighed.

"That's because he knows me pretty well, Buster! A lot better than you do! I'm no shrinking violet that has to be coddled and protected. In fact, I might just be tougher than both of you," Mary told him.

"You may be right at that," Johnny admitted.

"So, what the hell is the good news?"

"The good news is we just turned the cops on to Donlley, and we also think that Fabian Morales may be the one pulling his strings," Chandler told her.

"You think the cops didn't know about him?" Mary asked.

"I think that Luther might have worked for the Circle, and that when they fell, he managed to avoid being swept up in it, continuing to operate business as usual. I think Morales came on the scene and knew about Luther and became his new sponsor while trying to re-establish the Circle," Chandler explained.

"That is certainly a pretty good theory. But is it one you can prove?" Mary asked.

"That's what we want you to look into. You're better on the computers than either of us are. So, you run the cyber searches and we'll handle the street level stuff," Chandler explained.

"Fair enough. So, what are you to going to do now?" Mary asked.

"We are going to hit the streets and see what we can turn up. I think it might be time for us to go rattle Fabian Morales' cage."

"That sound like a plan," Johnny grinned showing bright white teeth.

"Then go do it. I'll see if I can find anything linking

the two."

~ ~ ~

The rain continued to fall as Chandler and Quick headed out to the Jeep Cherokee. They got inside. "How you want to do this?" Quick asked.

"I'm going in my capacity as an investigator for Arnie Grossman's defense, and you are my associate," Chandler shrugged.

"So, you going to do the heavy lifting?"

"Unless he has bodyguards that strenuously object to our line of questioning. If that happens, I hope you will intervene."

"I like intervening," Johnny smiled.

"I thought that you might," Chandler said as he pulled out into traffic and headed north towards Fishers where Morales had both his home and offices. He figured they would swing by the offices first. If Morales wasn't there, they would move on to his home to beard the lion in his den.

Fabian Morales was in his office. He was still angry with Luther Donlley as he looked out his window at the gray clouds and the water streaming in rivulets down the glass of the window. He had no doubt that Sanchez would carry out his wishes. Enrico Sanchez controlled all of the Hispanic gangs in Indianapolis. A man named Gary Glick controlled the white gangs. All of them owed allegiance to Fabian Morales in one fashion or another. He had made it a point to cultivate them, to bring them under his umbrella of protection.

Since Luther had been showing signs of rebellion, he had to be dealt with. Morales methods would be harsh, but they would send a message that Luther couldn't ignore.

~ ~ ~

Enrico Sanchez had parked just off of east 10th street and Rural. He had managed to find pictures of Luther Donlley's immediate family. He knew exactly who he wanted to hit. Luther had a granddaughter named Darcy. From everything that Sanchez had been able to glean, Luther doted on the girl. That made her the perfect target in Sanchez's reckoning. He would watch for her, and when the opportunity arrived, he would take her and then he would have fun before leaving her corpse where Luther couldn't help but find out about it.

~ ~ ~

Darcy Donlley finished her chores. Mama had told her to relax, maybe go for a walk. She liked that idea. She needed to get out of the house, away from the tension that had the place in its grip since the two men had been there this morning. She pulled on a jacket since it was still raining, and headed out the door.

The air outside had cooled with the rain, and Darcy was glad for it. The humidity was not as bad under the cloudy sky. She hoped that the sun would remain behind the clouds until it set. The rain was cold but refreshing. She walked to the end of the block and turned up a side street. She was not prepared when strong hands grabbed her from behind and pulled her down to the ground.

~ ~ ~

"This guy didn't spare any expense on this place," Johnny Quick whistled as Chandler guided the Cherokee up the long drive to the rather ostentatious mansion that served as Fabian Morales' home. Both men took note of the private army of suit-clad gunmen surrounding the house.

"We might want to rethink our approach."

"Maybe, maybe not," Chandler shrugged as he drove around the circular drive in front of the house, stopping in front of the front doors of the house. Chandler shut off the engine and opened his door. Johnny shook his head, frowning as he followed suit. There were times working with Chandler was really hard on the nerves. He followed him up the front steps.

The thick double doors opened at their approach and a butler in full livery awaited them. "Mr. Morales is expecting you," he said.

"Thanks," Chandler told him. They stepped inside and the butler shut the door behind them.

"This way, please," the man said, leading them deeper into the house. Johnny Quick shook his head. He certainly had not expected a white, English butler. He wondered if the irony was lost on Chandler. That of a Mexican millionaire having an English butler.

Finally, they stopped in front of a pair of heavy oak doors. The butler rapped on them sharply with his fist. A voice inside called out and the butler turned the knobs and opened the doors so that Chandler and Quick could enter. Once they had, he silently closed the heavy doors behind them.

Fabian Morales stood as they entered, stepping around his desk and walking forward to shake hands. He shook hands with them both and turned and walked back behind his desk and sat down. "How may I help you, Mr. Chandler?"

"I know you spoke to my associate Ms. Norman yesterday, but I have some follow-up questions," Chandler replied.

"Certainly. Anything to help poor Arnie," Morales smiled, interlocking his fingers as he put his elbows on the desk.

"Are you sure you really want to help Arnie?" Chandler asked.

"Whatever do you mean?"

"Here's what I think, Fabian. I think that maybe you needed Arnie's cash to get this project off the ground, and you knew that he could bring in other investors. But, you didn't like being left in the background as Arnie became the face of the project. I've looked into your past, you see. I know all about your past, the stuff that doesn't make the official biography. I think maybe you are trying to establish a power base here in Indianapolis using the city's gangs and Arnie is your fall guy," Chandler said, laying it all out for Morales.

Quick was watching the man's reaction to Chandler's words. It was obvious that Morales was getting angry, his face flushed with anger and his eyes flared with rage.

"Get out of my house!" Morales was on his feet, his fists balled in rage, spittle flying from his mouth with every word.

"What's the matter, Fabian? Did I hit a nerve?" Chandler asked a grin on his face. Quick had a hand under his jacket near the butt of his Ruger GP-100, ready for anything.

"Get out!" Morales roared, his whole body shaking.

"I think we done wore out our welcome," Johnny

said softly, touching Chandler on the shoulder.

"I think you might be right," Chandler agreed as they backed to the doors. Johnny opened the doors, not taking his hand off the grip of his gun. He and Chandler passed through it and shut it behind him.

"I suggest we beat some feet," Johnny said.

"I think that's a good idea," Chandler said as they raced through the mansion to the front door. They stepped outside and climbed into the Jeep Cherokee and Chandler fired up the engine. He had the Jeep rolling as the outside security started to scramble towards them. Johnny drew his weapon and rolled down his window as Chandler sped towards the gate.

Some of the men opened fire at them. Bullets pinged off the body as Chandler aimed for the gates. They were starting to rumble closed and a guy stepped out of the guard shake with a shotgun. He lifted it to his shoulder, aiming at them. Johnny fired his revolver and the guard jerked back, the shotgun flying from his hands.

The jeep hit the gates, knocked them askew, and was through with the sound of tearing metal. Then it was in the street and speeding away. "That was damn close," Johnny sighed.

"It was closer than I like, but we hit pay dirt. Fabian Morales was behind the death of Tiffany Mendez, even if he didn't kill her," Chandler said.

"All we need now is proof," Johnny sighed.

"We'll get it, Pal. You can count on that," Chandler told him.

~ ~ ~

Fabian Morales was in a rage! How had Chandler

figured it out? The private investigator and his woman had to die! So, did the black man, whoever he was! They could destroy him, ruin his plans to rebuild the Circle before he had even gotten it off the ground. More importantly, they could prove that Arnie Grossman hadn't killed the girl.

He hoped that Sanchez had sent his message to Luther. He would need all of the gangs in order to make sure that Chandler did not survive to expose his plans!

~ ~ ~

Blue King was walking down the alley when he saw something. He wasn't sure exactly what it was. An old bundle of clothes? He moved forward. It was a body. A girl. Her clothes had been shredded and there was blood all over her and the alley. He had seen dead bodies before. He knelt down next to her, then he gagged and turned away, making it to the other side of the alley before vomiting all the contents from his stomach.

He recognized the bloody face that stared upward at the sky. What he hadn't been prepared for was the mutilation. Her breasts had been cut off and lay on the ground beside her. Her stomach had been cut open and her female organs lay on the ground as well.

Blue staggered to his feet and headed for Luther's house. Luther was going to want to know about this. He pulled out his phone and dialed 9-1-1. When the dispatcher answered, he gave the location of the body and hung up. He had to tell Luther and hope that the man didn't kill him for bringing the bad news.

~ ~ ~

Alejandro Cruz and Steve Dickerson were the first detectives on the scene. They looked at the body as the uniforms strung out crime scene tape to block off the alley. "She got any ID on her?" Dickerson asked. Alejandro knelt down beside her and checked her pockets. He came up with an ID card. It had a picture of a pretty young woman on it, and a name. Darcy Donlley. Alejandro blew out air. He looked at Dickerson.

"Shit," he said.

"Shit?" Dickerson asked.

"The name, Steve. Darcy Donlley. I'll bet my eye teeth that she's related to Luther Donlley, the guy we were told runs all of the black gangs in town," Cruz sighed.

"Oh, shit!" Dickerson sighed.

Chapter Sixteen

Blue King staggered into Luther Donlley's house. He was out of breath and could barely stand. "Are you all right, Blue?" Annette Donlley asked him as she hurried to where he had stopped to rest.

"No, Miss Annette I ain't. I got to see Luther right away," Blue gasped, not wanting to tell Annette that her daughter had been murdered and mutilated. He really didn't want to be the one to tell Luther, but he knew the man would kill him if he got the news from anybody else!

"All right, just follow me," Annette said, throwing worried looks over her shoulder at him as she led him down the hall to the living room where Luther watched TV and held court. "Luther, Blue here has some news for you," she said.

"Speak boy," Luther looked up at him. Luther knew that the news couldn't be good from the look on Blue's face.

"It's about Darcy," Blue gasped, still fighting to get his breathing under control. Luther sat up straight in his chair, and he heard Annette gasp from behind him.

"What about Darcy, Blue?" Luther asked, his soft, yet with a brittle tone.

"She's dead, Luther. Someone done kilt her and cut her up in an alley a couple of blocks from here," Blue told him, his voice quivering and his knees shaking. His normally dark skin looked gray as he delivered the news.

"My Baby!" Annette wailed as she slumped to her knees, leaning against the doorway. Luther sat very still for at least a minute as he digested the news.

"You see anybody around when you find her?" Luther's voice was cold, colder than blue had ever heard it. A chill ran down his spine.

"No, Sir! Not a soul. It was pretty horrible," Blue almost whispered.

"You done good, telling me Boy."

"I hope so, Luther. I really do," Blue whispered.

"Did you call the po-lice?"

"Yes, Sir I did."

"You done good, Blue. I want you to get on the phone. I want all the chiefs here in an hour. I got a feeling that I know who is responsible," Luther said softly. He heaved himself out of his chair and walked over to Annette, kneeling beside her and putting his arms around his daughter to comfort her. Blue nodded and headed for another room to use the phone.

~ ~ ~

"Well, I think that could have gone better," Chandler said as he headed back towards the office.

"You think?" Johnny Quick looked over at him.

"I don't remember you objecting to the plan before we went in."

"Then you wasn't paying attention!"

"Call Larry, tell him to move Arnie to an undisclosed location. I have a feeling that he won't be safe at the Marriott much longer."

"I can do that," Johnny replied, pulling out his cell phone. He dialed Larry Sampson's number.

"Sampson and Wells, Attorneys at law," answered a prim voice.

"Johnny Quick for Mr. Sampson," Johnny told her.

"One moment please," the young woman's voice told him. Quick rolled his eyes as he watched the street. Chandler's driving was making him nervous.

"Johnny, how are you?" Larry Sampson's voice filled his ear.

"Chandler wants you to put Arnie Grossman somewhere safe and off the books," Johnny told him.

"Why?" Larry asked.

"Because Fabian Morales framed him, and he may want to tie up loose ends," Johnny explained.

"Okay, I'll get him moved. Tell Chandler to call me himself when he gets a chance," Sampson said.

"I'll pass it along," Johnny told him.

"Well?" Chandler looked over at him.

"He said he'd move him, and he wants you to call him as soon as possible," Johnny said.

"I'll do that," Chandler nodded.

~ ~ ~

Alejandro Cruz climbed out of his car and walked up the sidewalk to the front door of the house that Luther Donlley made home. He knocked loudly, stepping to the side on the off chance that someone might fire a gun through the door.

A woman appeared, her eyes red, her face tear-stained and puffy. "Can I help you?" she asked.

"I'm Detective Cruz, Metro PD. Is Annette or Luther Donlley present?"

"I'm Annette Donlley," she told him, straightening her back.

"I'm sorry to inform you that your daughter, Darcy Donlley is dead. She was murdered not far from here," Cruz told her.

"My baby," Annette staggered, nearly fainting.

Alejandro caught her and held her up. "I understand how hard this is," he told her.

"You ever lose a child?" she asked, looking into his eyes.

"No, I haven't," he told her honestly.

"Then you got no idea how I feeling!" Annette told him, tears running down her cheeks.

"I'll find the person that did this," Cruz told her.

"You better, or her grandfather will," Annette told him.

"Is he here?" Cruz asked, looking into her eyes.

"Nope. He done left to make arrangements for my baby girl."

"I am truly sorry for your loss, Mrs. Donlley."

"I doubt that Mr. Po-lice man. I doubt that very much," Annette said before turning away from him and stepping inside and slamming the door in his face. Cruz looked at the door. He guessed that he probably deserved that. He turned and made his way back down the walk to the car.

"How did that go?" Steve Dickerson asked.

"It could have gone better," Cruz sighed.

"Yeah," Dickerson nodded as he pulled their unmarked car out into traffic, heading back to the Metro station.

~ ~ ~

"You two don't look exactly happy," Mary observed as Chandler and Quick entered the office.

"That would be a fair observation," Chandler told her as he made a beeline to his office.

"You might want to lock that door," Johnny told her, nodding at the one they had just entered through.

"Okay," Mary stood and headed for the door, locking it and turning the sign from open to closed and then lowered the blinds and shut them. She followed the two men into the inner office and took a seat beside the one that Johnny Quick had settled into. "So, tell me what happened," Mary demanded.

"I found out that Fabian is definitely behind the dead girl at Arnie's house, and I'm pretty sure I know why," Chandler told her.

"That's good news, right?" Mary looked at him.

"It normally would be. Except I pushed him so hard, I'm pretty sure he's going to send people after us."

"I can see how that would be a problem."

"Yeah. I had Larry take Arnie someplace safe. Now I gotta figure out what to do about both Luther and Fabian."

"Can Alejandro help you?" Mary crossed her legs, one hand raised to let her chin rest on it.

"I hope so," Chandler told her.

~ ~ ~

Luther had gone to see what was left of his granddaughter in the alley. It told him who was responsible. He would stay away from the house for now. The cops would be going there soon enough to tell Annette what she already knew. That Darcy was dead, and that she had died hard and horribly.

Fabian Morales and his boys were going to pay for that! Fabian had wanted to send him a message. Well,

Luther was going to send a message right back. He was going to hurt Morales the way that Morales had hurt him. He was going to strike at family.

There was no way that Luther was going to let Morales get away with what he had done. The man had ambitions, ones that over-reached his abilities. Luther was going to show him how badly he had just fucked up!

~ ~ ~

"Find and kill those two!" Fabian Morales roared at his men.

"The girl is dead," Sanchez said as he entered the room.

"Forget about Luther right now. I want Chandler and his black sidekick dead! I want them dead now!" Morales screamed.

"That can be arranged, Jefe. However, I would not lose sight of what you just had me do to Luther Donlley's daughter. I don't believe that he will stand idly by," Sanchez warned.

"Luther is a dog, doing my bidding," Morales, sniffed. Sanchez gave him a worried look, wondering if his boss might not be losing it.

Sanchez had never seen Morales so angry as he was after his visit with the detective and his associate. Whatever they had said to him, had struck a deep wound. It might well have been one that had driven the boss over the edge. If that were the case, Fabian Morales was a danger to himself as well as others. If he proved too dangerous, Sanchez knew that he would have no choice but to gun his boss down like the rabid dog that he was turning into!

Morales turned, grumbling to himself as he turned

and walked out of the room. Sanchez watched him go, and he wondered if perhaps it wasn't too late!

~ ~ ~

Larry Sampson had grabbed Arnie Grossman and hurried him out to a waiting car. He figured that the farther he got Arnie from Indianapolis, the better. He gave the driver a location that was nearly fifty miles away, a small town off I-70 called New Castle, Indiana. The bad part was, he would have to accompany Arnie and make sure that his client didn't make any waves that might lead Fabian Morales to him.

Larry knew that was going to be a tough call. He would have to handle all communications for Arnie Grossman, whether Arnie liked it or not. He already knew that Arnie was NOT going to be a fan of it. That was okay, though. Because he knew that Chandler would find a way to take care of them, regardless.

~ ~ ~

"How do you want to handle this?" Mary looked at Chandler.

"I figure that first we call Alejandro and see what help he can give us. After that, we prepare for everything that our enemy can do. It might not necessarily be what they might do, but it will still give us an edge," Chandler told her.

"In other words, you've got nothing," Mary said flatly.

"Something like that," Chandler shrugged.

"That's about what I figured," Mary rolled her eyes.

"I never said it was the best plan," Chandler said.

"Because it wasn't," Mary shrugged.

"No, it wasn't."

~ ~ ~

Alejandro Cruz and Steve Dickerson had just got back to their desks when the telephone rang. Cruz picked up. "Alejandro, how's tricks?" Chandler's voice filled his ear.

"Well, somebody brutally murdered Luther Donlley's granddaughter. Got any ideas who might have done that?" Cruz growled into the phone.

"Shit! That's not good."

"Murder never is."

"I'm pretty sure it was Fabian Morales or one of his men. They were also the ones that were responsible for the death of Tiffany Mendez," Chandler explained.

"How is Morales mixed up in this?" Cruz demanded.

"I'm pretty sure that he's trying to rebuild The Circle, using all the gangs in town as his private army."

"That's a big leap, Chandler."

"Not really, considering after I confronted him his men tried to kill me."

"Yes, I'd call that evidence of the fact that Morales doesn't like you," Cruz shook his head.

"Luther must have stood up to Morales and Morales ordered the granddaughter killed to send him a message," Chandler said.

"That message is about to start a gang war in our town."

"Then we need to find a way to take them both down before things get out of hand."

"I'm afraid things have already gotten out of hand," Cruz sighed.

Chapter Seventeen

"What did Alejandro have to say?" Mary asked as Chandler hung up the phone.

"That we have a gang war starting," Chandler said softly.

"That can't be good," Mary said.

"It's not," Johnny cut in. "What happened?"

"It appears that Fabian got upset with Luther and sent someone to kill his granddaughter. Luther got the message that Fabian was sending and has called in all his troops to send a message back," Chandler explained.

"Well Fuck!" Johnny hissed.

"Pretty much. Plus, both sides are shooting for us as well."

"That gonna make it hard to get in the street to do anything to stop it."

"I'm not going into hiding," Chandler shrugged.

"Yeah, I didn't figure you would," Quick sighed.

"I'm not going into hiding either," Mary glared at them both.

"Then we do it together," Chandler said.

"And we hope for the best," Johnny Quick sighed.

~ ~ ~

"Why the fuck do we have to go to this little horseshit town, Larry?" Arnie Grossman groused from the passenger seat.

"Tell me, Arnie. Do you want to live or die?" Larry asked.

"I want to live, of course," Arnie shook his head.

"Then shut the fuck up and do what I tell you. Chandler found out that Fabian Morales was behind the dead girl that turned up in your house."

"Fabian? Why the hell would he do something like that?"

"Because he needed your money to get his project off the ground, and then he needed a scapegoat so that he could take over the project. Guess who he had figured to be the scapegoat?"

"Fabian did that to me?"

"Now you are getting the picture. Fabian was sending someone out to kill you, Arnie. If you were dead, you can't testify against him."

"Well fuck," Arnie leaned against his door.

"Exactly. You need to lay low and let Chandler handle this. I'm with you to make sure that this happens," Larry told him. Larry got off at the New Castle exit and headed north on State road 3. They went to Wal-Mart first, so that Arnie could grab a couple of bottles of vodka and some mixers, and then they crossed Highway 3 to the Steve Alford motel. Larry registered them in a room in his name. He hoped that Fabian Morales wouldn't think to look for him.

~ ~ ~

"So, what do we do first?" Johnny asked.

"I think that we should offer to help Luther," Chandler replied.

"Why?"

"We pissed him off, but not as much as we pissed off Morales. We help Luther, he will be the more forgiving of the two."

"You think so?"

"I do."

"You got balls, Chandler. I gotta say it," Johnny told him.

"He's got more than that," Mary said mischievously.

"That's too much information, Mary," Johnny told her.

"Maybe so, but it is true!"

"Guys, I'm right here," Chandler told them both. Both of them looked at him and grinned.

"We're aware," Mary gave him a broad wink.

"We need to gear up, and then we'll go see if Luther will talk to us," Chandler said. Mary and Quick nodded.

~ ~ ~

Nico Rodriguez and his crew were just walking out of a Mexican restaurant on the west side when gunfire ripped into the Mexican Mafia leader. Soon, they were just bleeding corpses on the sidewalk. Screams sounded from inside the restaurant and more wounded and dead were left wondering what had happened.

~ ~ ~

Travon Carlyle and Mickey C-note stepped out of a market on 10th and Rural when they were ripped to pieces by automatic weapons fire. The glass windows of the market shattered as bullets tore through it, shredding produce and killing innocents. The war had started.

~ ~ ~

"I'm sorry John, but I think we need to remove Fabian from the project. I've been doing some digging and Fabian is not as squeaky clean as he led us to believe. In fact, he has contacts with every street gang in the city," Ogden Spears said.

"It sounds like he fooled us all, Ogden," John Irwin said as he leaned back in his seat.

"I think he is trying to rebuild The Circle, John."

"That would not be good for the city. It took us a while to recover from the exposure and destruction of the original Circle, and what it did to our home."

"No, it would not. That detective, Chandler, told me that he believes that Fabian had something to do with that dead woman turning up at Arnie's house. I say that we continue to back Arnie, and I'll see if I can find other investors to replace Fabian Morales."

"I think that would be a good idea," John Irwin said.

"So, then we are in agreement?" Ogden Spears asked.

"We are as far as I'm concerned. You contact the others and see what they have to say," Irwin told him.

~ ~ ~

"Motherfuck!" Steve Dickerson yelled as word of three more drive by shootings came in. The homicide unit was being stretched thin by the growing war between the black and Hispanic gangs. So far, the white gangs were staying out of it, preferring that their enemies eliminate each other.

"Yeah, c'mon we need to roll on this one," Alejandro Cruz growled as he grabbed his coat.

"Where to?"

"A market at Rural and 10th."

"That's not far from Luther's house."

"Exactly," Cruz shot back over his shoulder as he headed out the door.

~ ~ ~

"So how you want to play this?" Johnny Quick asked, his eyes searching the sidewalks as Chandler cruised down 10th street.

"Mary stays with the car, ready to get us the hell away from there in case we need to come out in a hurry. You come in with me to watch my back while I try to talk Luther into stopping this war," Chandler explained.

"As a plan, that really sucks," Mary told him.

"Have you got a better one?" Chandler looked at her.

"Not really, no."

"Then we go with mine," Chandler said. He pulled to the curb outside Luther Donlley's house. Five beefy young black studs sat on the porch. They all had on coats no doubt to hide their guns. They eyed the green Jeep Cherokee as it parked. Chandler and Johnny got out, and Mary moved to the driver's seat. She kept the engine running as the two of them started up the walk.

The five young bloods stood up as they approached. "Luther been looking for you two," one of them said.

"Then go tell him we're here. We want to parley," Chandler told him.

"Parley?" the kid looked befuddled.

"Talk," Johnny put in, shaking his head. He had to wonder just how ignorant these kids were.

"Right," the kid said, and then he disappeared inside. A few moments lather Luther Donlley stepped out onto the front porch.

"What the hell are you two doing back here?" he demanded.

"We heard about what Morales had done to your granddaughter and we are here to help," Chandler told him.

"How exactly do you planning on doing that?" Luther demanded.

"I'm going to take Fabian Morales down one way or another. I just need you to answer one question for me," Chandler told him.

"What's that?" Luther asked guardedly.

"Did you kill Tiffany Mendez and dump her in Arnie Grossman's house?" Chandler asked.

"Had no part in killing that girl. He called and asked for some of my boys to dump the body," Luther admitted.

"That's what I needed to know. Call your army back off the streets, Luther, and I promise I will get justice for your granddaughter," Chandler said.

'You mean you gonna turn him over to the po-lice."

"Nope. I said justice, Luther. You think on it, you'll know what I mean."

"Who the fuck are you?"

"I'm Fabian Morales worst nightmare," Chandler replied with a tight smile.

"You got twenty-four hours. Then I go after that psycho myself," Luther told him.

"I'll get him," Chandler promised. Then he and Johnny walked backwards down the walk and got back in the Jeep. Mary pulled away from the curb and headed west.

"That went better than I expected," Mary told him.

"Better than I expected it to go as well," Johnny added.

"Luther has checked me out. He knows my reputation," Chandler shrugged.

"You think that's gonna be enough to make sure he does what he says he'll do?" Johnny asked.

"Luther's that kind of guy. He didn't keep his word, he'd been dead a long time ago. That's how he's managed to keep control of the black gangs."

"I get the feeling that you think leaving him in charge might be a good thing," Mary observed.

"Something like that. Sometimes it's better have the devil you know than one you don't," Chandler told her.

"He's right," Johnny added.

"I suppose I shouldn't be surprised that you agree with him."

"You shouldn't. You talk to Cruz, now that he knows about Luther, he tell you the same thing," Johnny told her.

"One of these days, I'm going to crack this man code that you all share," Mary told them both.

~ ~ ~

Fabian Morales poured himself a drink. He wasn't liking the news that was coming his way. Five of his crews had been taken out. Plus, he was hearing rumbles that he was being cut out of the city center projects. Ogden Spears had threatened him, so perhaps it was time for Ogden Spears to die!

"Sanchez!" he roared. In seconds, his top hit man was standing in front of him.

"You called, Sir?" Sanchez asked.

"Ogden Spears needs to die. Make it happen," Morales said.

"I can do that. What about the two men that were here earlier?"

"Find them and kill them. Surely, they can't be hiding, not with all of our boys out on the street?"

"They will be found and taken care of, Jefe. I will make sure of it," Sanchez told him.

Chapter Eighteen

"Where to now?" Mary asked as they drove aimlessly through the downtown area.

"We need to draw Fabian Morales out of his mansion. He's in a fortress there," Chandler said.

"How do you propose we do that?" Johnny asked, his eyes sweeping the streets for danger.

"I'm still working on that," Chandler admitted. His cell phone rang. He pulled it out and looked at it. "Ogden Spears," he said before answering. "Hello?"

"Mr. Chandler?" Spears asked.

"Yeah, Mr. Spears. What can I do for you?"

"I believe you. Fabian Morales is trying to rebuild the circle. I have ousted him from the project, and I think that he may well try to kill me," Spears explained.

"I think you are probably right. Where are you now?" Chandler asked.

"At my home, of course," Spears replied, his tone uncertain.

"I'm on my way. Don't answer the door for anybody but me. I'm going to send the police to your home to set up a defensive perimeter. I agree that your life is in real danger," Chandler told him.

"I'll lock all the doors and set the alarms," Spears said.

"I'll be there shortly," Chandler told him and broke the connection. He immediately dialed Alejandro Cruz's cell.

"What the hell do you want, Chandler? I'm knee deep in homicides at the moment," Cruz growled at him.

"I got Luther to give me 24 hours to take down Fabian Morales. Also, Ogden Spears ousted Morales from the project, and he's pretty sure Morales will send people to kill him. Can you send a couple of cars until I can get to him?" Chandler asked.

"Yeah, I can probably do that," Cruz replied.

"Thanks," Chandler told him, hanging up. He looked at Mary. "Head for Ogden Spear's place."

~ ~ ~

Sanchez had Camino and Gutierrez with him as he approached the home of Ogden Spears. His plan was a simple one. They would force their way in, kill Ogden Spears, and then sever his head and take it back to Mr. Morales.

If the police were there, they would cut them down like wheat before a scythe. Sanchez smiled at the imagery. It was amusing to him. He didn't care what the world might think. He was loyal to his Jefe. He would complete the mission that he had been sent on.

~ ~ ~

Mary drove quickly through the streets, heading for Fishers where Ogden Spears lived. She figured out shortcuts that Chandler never knew existed. They got to Spears place before the cops did. Mary parked and then the three of them headed inside, bringing their weapons along.

"Thank you for coming," Spears greeted them.

"Glad to help Ogden."

"I'm really worried," Spears said.

"You should be. Morales has lost it," Chandler told him.

"I suspected that when he threatened me."

"That would be a good indicator."

"We will protect you. But we need your help to do it."

"What can I do?"

"When we stop the hit team, I need you to call Fabian."

"I can do that," Spears replied.

~ ~ ~

Sanchez guided his vehicle up the driveway. There were two Metro P.D. cars waiting. One of the officers climbed out. Camino opened fire, cutting the first one down. The other cops opened fire. Sanchez cursed. This was not going as planned! His men opened fire as well, targeting the police cars. The officers did not survive the engagement.

Sanchez and his men exited the car and approached the house. They were very surprised when a shotgun opened up on them, taking them out two at a time. Soon they were dead on the grass.

Chandler walked out from the corner of the house. Johnny rounded the other corner and Mary opened the front door. And she and Ogden Spears stepped outside onto the front porch. Spears looked like he was about to faint. "That was brutal," he gasped.

"It was, but would you rather that we let them get here first and kill you?" Chandler looked at him.

"N-no," Spears stammered.

"Johnny, get the keys and unlock the trunk. We're about to send Fabian Morales a message of our own,"

Chandler said.

"What are you going to do?" Spears asked.

"It's probably better if you don't know, Ogden. Mary will stay here to protect you, though I doubt if you'll have any more visitors from Morales' camp."

"Okay," Spears said, turning and hurrying back inside.

"Chandler," Mary started.

"No buts, Kid. He needs you here and Johnny and I are going to be really busy for the next couple of hours," Chandler cut her off!

"We will be discussing this later," Mary told him, her voice icy cold.

"I figured that already," Chandler told her as he began to help Johnny stuff dead bodies into the trunk of the car. Mary went back inside the house, the door slamming behind her.

"I think I hate to be you once this is over," Johnny told him.

"Yeah, I think you're right," Chandler sighed.

~ ~ ~

Fabian Morales paced back and forth in his study. He had decided that he was probably safer in his home this evening than going out. Luther had hit several of his people earlier, but for the moment, the streets had become amazingly quiet. It bothered him. Luther had pulled his people back. Why? He hated not knowing. It was eating him up inside and making him crazy.

"Boss, we just found Sanchez's car outside the gate. It was running but there was nobody inside it," Jesus De Cordova, his second in command announced as he entered the study.

"Is the car wired?" Morales asked.

"Not that we can tell."

"Bring it inside, but leave it on the drive and check it out," Morales ordered, thankful to be able to give orders about something at last. And Jesus, have one of your men drive it in."

"Si, Jefe," De Cordova replied, exiting the room. Morales walked to his desk and pulled out a Beretta 92-F, once the main pistol of the United States Armed Forces. He stuffed it into his waistband as he walked towards the front door of the mansion.

Ernie Valdez climbed slowly into the car, gingerly closing the door and putting the vehicle in drive. He was relieved when it didn't explode like he had expected it to. He carefully guided it inside the gate, just far enough that the gates could close behind it and then he shut off the motor and got the hell out of the car. Fabian Morales was making his way down the driveway toward them.

"Open the trunk, Ernie," De Cordova ordered. Gingerly, Ernie made his way to the trunk and inserted the key, unlocking it and raising the lid up. He saw inside and then spun away, puking his guts out.

De Cordova walked up and looked inside, and his face went pale, but he managed to keep from throwing up. A shotgun does terrible things to a human body, especially a short-barreled one. The men inside the trunk had been blown to pieces. A note had been left on top of them.

"Welcome to the jungle," the note read. Fabian Morales saw it and went ballistic!

"This was Chandler and the nigger!" he screamed.

Put more men on the streets, find them!" Morales screamed. Just then, De Cordova's head exploded under the impact of a high-velocity round. Blood and brains splattered on Fabian Morales' face. The big man hit the ground and more rounds thundered into his compound. The garage beside the house exploded in a ball of flame, the concussion knocking all of his men to the ground.

Morales fought his way to his feet and began firing into the darkness with no real target. Ernie Valdez tackled him to the ground, knocking the gun out of his fist. He had the other soldiers surround them in a run to the house. Two more men died under a sniper's fire before they made it inside.

~ ~ ~

"How long do you figure we got before the cops arrive?" Johnny asked as he picked up Chandler in the Cherokee and sped away from the scene.

"Long enough. Fabian has a Meth lab set up in Avon. I suggest we go there next," Chandler replied.

"Okay, it sounds like you have a plan," Johnny admitted.

"I do. I plan to hit him where it hurts, where the money comes from," Chandler replied.

~ ~ ~

Fabian was nearly foaming at the mouth once he was safe inside his mansion. "Forget about the niggers! I want Phillip Chandler and his sidekick dead!" he screamed, spittle flying from his lips.

"I've sent the word out Boss," Ernie told him. After Jesus' death, he had found himself promoted to head cock of the walk through the process of attrition.

"I want his head on a stick before dawn," Morales

growled.

"I'm working on it," Ernie assured him. But Ernie was getting nervous. The boss was losing it. He was about to crack under the pressures that were piling up on top of him. Ernie had no wish to die alongside him.

Calls were already coming in from Mexico wondering why there was so much in the news about Indiana. Ernie was handling them as best he could, but he knew that the leaders of the cartel had decided that Fabian Morales was becoming a liability.

Ernie could see the writing on the wall, and he knew that when the time came, it would be up to him to pull the trigger on his boss. It wasn't something that he was looking forward to.

Chapter Nineteen

Fabian Morales had a stash house and cutting operation in Avon, Indiana. It was in a relatively small ranch style house that was isolated in a small woods just at the edge of the city limits. It had a gate at the end of the long and winding gravel drive. Chandler pulled the Cherokee over to the side of the road and slipped out. Darkness had settled heavily and the wind carried the smell of rain. Thunder rumbled deeply in the clouds overhead.

Johnny reached into the back of the Cherokee and came out with an AK-47 that he had taken from a gangbanger. He checked the magazine and it was seated properly, and then pulled back the bolt. He moved the fire selector to three-round bursts.

Chandler held the Mossberg 500 "Persuader" 12-guage pump with the extended 7-round magazine. Together they silently approached the building. "You smell that?" Johnny asked.

Chandler nodded. "Yeah, they are cooking meth in there," Chandler replied softly, his voice barely a whisper.

"So how you want to do this?" Johnny asked.

"You take the front, I'll go in from the back, we squeeze them in the middle, get them outside and then we burn their house down," Chandler shrugged.

"It's a plan," Johnny admitted.

"You got a better one?"

"Not really, no."

"See you inside," Chandler said before drifting away, becoming just another shadow in the night. Johnny ducked below window level as he approached the front door. He wanted to keep the element of surprise on their side. He could hear laughter from inside, along with some gutter Spanish. Yep, they boys belonged to Morales all right.

Johnny reached the front door without being seen. He stood to his full height and took a deep breath in and let it out slow. He snuck a glance at his watch. Chandler had plenty of time to get to the back door by now. He lifted his foot and slammed his boot against the door near the knob. The lock shattered as the door flew open. Johnny stepped inside. Two men spun towards him, both going for guns tucked into their waistbands. Johnny cut loose with the Ak-47, dropping them. He moved deeper into the house.

~ ~ ~

Chandler had worked his way around to the back door. There was a guy outside smoking a cigarette. Chandler knelt and put the shotgun on the ground, drawing his Schrade assisted opening spear point knife from his pocket. He gripped the knife in his hand as he slithered closer. One hand shot out, covering the man's mouth as the blade snickted open and locked in place. Chandler drove the blade into his kidney, twisting it and causing a sudden and total renal failure. He lowered the dead man to the ground, wiping the blade off on the dead man's clothing. He pushed the blade back into the handle and put it back into his pocket, picking up the shotgun as he did so.

He heard Johnny kick open the front door and then he did the same to the back door. He let the muzzle of the shotgun enter first, firing at the first man he saw with a gun. The charge of double-ought buckshot caught the man in the middle and nearly split him in half. Chandler worked the pump as he moved deeper inside. There were two skinny women who were obviously there to help with the cooking, though it was obvious that they both used the methamphetamine as well. Johnny shooed them outside.

Chandler quickly created a fuse that would ignite the chemicals used to make the drug and then he and Johnny vacated the house. By the time they got outside, the two women were long gone. Chandler and Johnny had just reached the Cherokee when the building exploded in a ball of flame.

Chandler looked at Johnny. "Time to call Fabian," he grinned.

"He not going to be a happy camper," Johnny grinned back.

"I'm counting on it," Chandler said.

~ ~ ~

"Boss, we just got word that the house in Avon was blown up," Ernie Valdez announced as he entered the study.

"*Madre Dios*! It had to be Chandler," Morales swore.

"Boss, there was more than a million bucks stashed in that house. It's all gone now," Ernie said softly.

"Why isn't Chandler dead already?" Morales demanded.

"Because he's good, Boss," Ernie replied.

157

"You mean that he is better than you and your boys?" Morales looked at him.

~ ~ ~

"All of the black gang members have vanished off the streets," Steve Dickerson said.

"That is some good news at least," Alejandro Cruz sighed.

"It is, but the Mexican gang bangers are cruising around looking pissed."

"Have the uniforms start arresting them for anything they can think off. If we can get them off the streets too, we can keep this from getting any worse," Cruz told him.

"I hope you're right," Dickerson replied.

~ ~ ~

"Fabian, how's it hanging," Chandler asked when the Morales answered the telephone.

"I'm going to kill you, Chandler," Fabian Morales told him vehemently.

"Then meet me on the Canal River Walk at dawn," Chandler said. "And Fabian, come alone. It will be just the two of us, man to man."

"Si, I agree to that. I will kill you, Chandler. And then the city will be mine."

"Indianapolis will never belong to you, Fabian. It's too good for the likes of you," Chandler replied before hanging up. He looked over at Johnny. "Let's go get set up."

"Sho' thing, Boss," Johnny grinned.

~ ~ ~

4:15 A.M.

Chandler and Quick had set up at opposite ends of

the White River Park Canal Walk. They would know when Fabian Morales and his men showed up. It was cloudy and humid, the temperature a balmy and sticky 72 degrees. With the cloud cover and the storm coming, it would not get any lighter until about seven o'clock. The storm was their friend, helping provide concealment from the men that were coming to kill them.

The thunder got louder and before long, fat drops of rain began to fall. Chandler was glad of the ball cap on his head, the brim shielding his eyes from the driving rain. Morales would be coming soon, and then they could end this thing.

The original Circle had been a cancer that had been eating the city alive before Chandler had broken the secret second government of the Circle City. A group of wealthy men and women running the criminals from the shadows, brought down because they had murdered the wrong hooker. That had almost been poetic.

That was when he had met Mary Norman. She had come into the Slippery Noodle where he was a sometime bouncer and hired him to find her friend who had disappeared after working a private party. A crooked cop had worked Mary over, but Chandler rescued her and found her friend's killer and had brought the Circle crashing down.

He would not allow Fabian Morales to rebuild that organization. He would die before he allowed that to happen!

~ ~ ~

Johnny Quick sighed as the rain started. He hated the rain. It reminded him too much of time spent fighting in South American jungles a few years back as part of the so-called war on drugs. It hadn't taken long for him to figure out that the CIA and other shadow agencies were using the Cartels to finance their black budgets away from government oversight.

He had quit in disgust and headed home to Detroit where he had found work as an enforcer for the local Mafia Don. He had a good gig there, until they tried to frame the basketball player for a murder that he didn't commit. Johnny had liked the kid, respected him a lot more than the guys on the team that were shaving points for his boss. When Chandler had come around looking into the frame up, Johnny saw a man like himself. Someone who did what they said they would do and who did it for the right reasons. So, he had jumped ship and helped Chandler clear the kid.

Of course, he could never go back to Detroit, because there was a price on his head if he were to ever try. But as long as he stayed in Indiana, his old boss would leave him alone. He and Chandler had become friends because they respected each other. Now, each was willing to die for the other. That was something that Mary would never understand. It was a part of the man code, the brotherhood of warriors.

A sound caught his attention. A car engine, no, two of them approaching fast. "They are coming," he keyed his radio mike.

"Then let's end this," Chandler replied.

"Yas suh," Quick replied, flashing a wide, white-toothed grin as he watched two cars pull to a stop and several heavily armed men climbed out. Johnny watched as they spread out in a skirmish line and headed into the park. He spotted Morales hanging back about five yards behind his men. That figured. Morales wasn't enough of a leader to lead from the front. He was a coward who put his men out front to die for him so he would have time to run away from any real danger.

Johnny smiled. He was going to cut that option off. He stood and started to move, getting behind the line of men and heading for their vehicles. These boys were about to find out what kind of hell that war really was!

~ ~ ~

Chandler waited until he knew that Morales hadn't sent men in from his end of the park before he started to move. He was like a ghost in the shadows, moving silently through the pouring rain that pelted down from the sky. Thunder rumbled above him.

Chandler slid along the canal, avoiding the lights placed along the sidewalks so he didn't present a silhouette against them that would be a target for his enemies. Chandler crouched behind a bush, his knife gripped tightly in his hand. A man stepped past him. Chandler moved in behind him, his hand clamping over the man's mouth as he drove the blade into his kidney and twisted it, causing instant renal failure. He pulled the blade out and slit his throat to be on the safe side. Chandler lowered him to the ground and began stalking his next target.

~ ~ ~

Johnny Quick sprinted away from the cars and found concealment behind some bushes. A heartbeat later, the cars exploded in a bright white fireball that lifted them both into the air and sent a shockwave into the park, causing men to stumble. Johnny lifted his AK and opened fire, spraying it towards where he had last seen Fabian Morales.

He heard screams as his bullets found yielding flesh and bone, and then he heard Chandler's gun open up as well. Lances of flame exploded out of the darkness and men fell and died. Screams ripped the early morning, along with pleas of mercy from the wounded and dying. Johnny quick grinned as he moved forward to finish the dying off.

~ ~ ~

Fabian Morales was frantic. Explosions behind him, his men screaming and dying around him. He had a pistol in hand, but had no idea where to shoot. How had this happened? How was it falling apart? He screamed his rage into the storm, but the storm paid little attention to his rage. It was striking with its own!

"Fabian," Chandler called softly. Ten yards separated the two men. Morales spun to face him.

"You!" the Mexican spat, his face nearly purple with rage.

"The Circle is dead, Fabian. I'll never let it be rebuilt," Chandler said.

"I will run this town," Morales screamed as he raised his pistol. Chandler drew his .45 from under his arm and fired. Fabian Morales head exploded. His body remained upright for a long moment, and then it toppled to the ground. Chandler holstered his automatic. The war was over. The Circle was finished for a second time. It was time to go home.

"You got him," Johnny said as he joined him.

"Yes, I did. But there will be others. Rich men never give up once they acquire a taste for power. There will always be those who want to climb to the top," Chandler said.

"And there will always be guys like us who won't let them," Johnny told him.

"I'm going to go get Mary and then go home," Chandler said.

"That, my friend, sounds like the best idea I have heard all day."

Chapter Twenty

One week later...

"Chandler, I need to thank you for clearing my name, and for exposing that rat Fabian," Arnie Grossman said.

"Arnie, the check you gave me was thanks enough," Chandler told the man as he sipped at a bottle of Killian's Red.

"We did appreciate the bonus," Mary added from her seat next to Chandler.

"Believe me, you guys earned it, as did Larry. I've put him on retainer."

"I'm sure that made Larry very happy," Chandler grinned, slipping his arm around Mary and pulling her close in a hug.

"Ogden managed to find some clean investors to replace Fabian Morales. But to be safe, I'd like the two of you to check them out and make sure they really are squeaky clean," Grossman told them.

"We can do that, Arnie. It won't be a problem."

"Just stop by the office and sign a contract first," Mary added.

"You hang onto this one Chandler. She's really got a head for business," Arnie told him.

"Yes, she does," Chandler agreed, leaning over and giving her a kiss.

"By the way, this is ginger ale. Larry got me into a program and I'm doing my best to give up the booze.

What happened to Tiffany, well, it opened my eyes. Going on the wagon seemed to be the right thing to do," Arnie told them.

"I'm glad to hear it, Arnie," Chandler clapped him on the back.

"Okay, I'm out of here. I have a meeting in the morning and then I've got some civic centers to build to help the underprivileged kids of Indianapolis. You guys have fun," Arnie told them as he tossed a twenty on the bar and headed out the door.

"He is a very interesting person," Mary observed as she watched him exit the building.

"He is. But Arnie is a good man. He's one who really loves helping the kids of this city. He will do a lot of good here," Chandler told her.

"I agree. You do a lot of good here too," Mary told him.

"I try."

"You do far more than try. You and Johnny, you two are a unique combination. You both have a code of honor that you follow. You both understand each other. Alejandro follows that same code, and he's part of it too. I may never understand it, but I do recognize it. It is a big part of why I love you as much as I do," Mary told him.

"I know that. You are the light of my life, Mary Norman. You are my reason for living. One of these days, I may even ask you to marry me," Chandler told her.

"When that day comes, Phillip, I will say yes," Mary told him, meaning it. He leaned forward and kissed her, and for a moment all was righ with the world.

❄ ❄ ❄

Thank you for reading.

Please review this book. Reviews help others find Absolutely Amazing eBooks and inspire us to keep providing these marvelous tales.

If you would like to be put on our email list to receive updates on new releases, contests, and promotions, please go to AbsolutelyAmazingEbooks.com and sign up.

About the Author

Bill Craig taught himself to read at age four and began writing his own stories at age six. He published his first novel at age 40 and says it only took him 34 years to become an overnight success! He has been publishing steadily ever since that first book *Valley of Death* and now has 80 books in print or ebook. Bill is the proud father of four children ranging in age from 38 to almost 8. He has 7 grandchildren and 1 great grandchild. Mr. Craig has worked a wide variety of jobs over the years from private security and corrections work to being a grill cook and dishwasher. He has been a news reporter, done factory work and even a stint as a railroad clerk. He currently does customer service work to support his writing addiction. His ultimate goal in life is to break the record held by pulp author and creator of *The Shadow*, Walter B. Gibson, for writing the most works in a single year!

ABSOLUTELY AMA⚡ING eBOOKS

AbsolutelyAmazingEbooks.com
or AA-eBooks.com